# OFF THE HOOK

MINDY LEMIUEX

*Dedicated to Andy. You are my best friend, my biggest fan, and an amazing supporter. (But you'd make a terrible pirate, darling. I'm sorry.)*

# PROLOGUE

Three young adults stood next to two headstones in a dismal cemetery near an old brick church in England. The first of the three was a young woman in her early-20s. The other two were her brothers, both a year or two younger than she.

"Darling" was the surname on both headstones – the two parents of the three siblings who huddled next to each other, sharing one black umbrella under a dismal, drizzly sky.

Wendy, John, and Michael Darling had lost both parents to a carriage accident just the week before. Tears rolled down their faces, just as rain rolled down the grave markers. Wendy, whose arms were wrapped around her brothers as she stood between them, hugged them tighter to give them comfort, and to draw comfort from their presence.

None of the three saw a darkly dressed figure of

modest height move toward them. He came slowly, carefully, though there was no doubt that they were his destination. The figure, who appeared to be around Wendy's age, was initially noticed by Michael. At first, he thought nothing of it, until they were approached.

The figure, his hat pulled low over his green eyes, lifted his faintly cleft chin to reveal his face. Michael looked to Wendy. When he caught her eye, he tilted his head at the newcomer. Wendy followed Michael's indication. "Peter?" she whispered.

This caught John's attention. He stiffened upon seeing another person intruding on their solitude. When recognition hit, his whole being relaxed, and he strode forward to wrap Peter in a brotherly hug. Michael and Wendy followed a heartbeat later, and the four held each other wordlessly for several moments. Wendy let a sob loose.

"Hush there now," Peter coaxed soothingly, his British accent light. "You're not alone." He pulled back and faced the Darling siblings. "I am sorry about your parents," he said earnestly. "I mourn for you, and I wish to mourn with you."

The siblings looked at him curiously. He wished to mourn *with* them?

"This may be too soon to suggest, but listen: Come away with me to Neverland. Let the Lost Boys and I be your family. Let Neverland be your home. Heal in Neverland with us. Leave London and time behind. You know you have a place there as you once did. Come with me."

John looked at Michael, who looked at Wendy, who

was looking at Peter. Wendy's face held a combination of sorrow and reserve. But anyone who knew her could tell she was thinking. She was considering this idea of Peter's to leave behind England at the beginning of the 20<sup>th</sup> century. She looked up at her brothers, both now taller than she, and both of whom seemed determined. She could tell they were already set on this proposal. There was nothing left for them in London. With a silent nod from Wendy to John, he looked to Peter and said, "When do we leave?"

YEARS HAD PASSED since the Darling siblings returned to Neverland.

*Years*, thought Hook derisively. *Neverland doesn't have years. There's no accounting of time here.*

He'd been watching the debates between Peter and Wendy that happened more and more frequently. She wanted to return to "the real world," as she called it. Peter simply wanted to stay in Neverland forever, playing the hero and never having any worries other than where the next adventure lay.

Wendy had grown weary of his lifestyle. Her brothers seemed to feel the same way, seeing as how they stood resolutely next to Wendy each time she and Peter had those discussions. Somehow, she'd convinced him in the end.

Most of the Lost Boys wanted to leave, too. Wendy could be very persuasive, but not in a calculating way. That wasn't the way of Wendy Darling.

Hook's body (by appearance, in his mid-20s) sat huddled in the hold of Peter's ship – the ship that could fly between Neverland and whatever lay elsewhere. Hook was tired of this lifestyle, too. Wendy's arguments had hit him to the core and convinced him as well.

Never thinking to find himself as a stowaway in any situation, Hook smirked and chuckled to himself, lightly shaking his head, brushing his dark hair across his eyebrows. He didn't know what any of them would find once they landed, but it had to be better than the same thing over and over, day after day, being in Neverland. Never progressing, never growing, never knowing what else there could be.

He was literally sitting in the dark, and proverbially taking a leap into the dark, leaving Neverland. He was tired of the never-ending games between him and Peter. He was tired of being conniving; tired of being a villain. He wanted something more from his life – to change from villainy, learn a trade, start a family, grow older, and move on.

Not only was Wendy persuasive (as evidenced by her conversations with Peter), but she'd developed incredibly during the years she and her brothers had grown up in London. Her features were delicate, her blue eyes certain and intelligent, her hair long and honey-colored, her stature regal. He admired who she had become and hoped he could find someone like her wherever they landed and started over.

"Ready to fly, boys?" he heard Peter shout from the deck.

"Ready, Peter!" they shouted back.

The ship began to move and a few crates and boxes toppled over, nearly landing on Hook. He lifted his firm arms overhead and took hold of a beam to steady himself. He closed his deep blue eyes, took a breath, and felt ready to move forward with his life.

# 1

---

Peter was pulled from his reverie when a student a row over and three seats up sneezed. He sat in a large room, surrounded by other students who were huddled over their desks, number-two pencils in hand, working their way through end-of-term exams.

He'd been thinking about the day he left Neverland for good and wondered (for the umpteenth time) how in the world they'd landed the ship in this place and at this time of Earth's history. Last he'd checked, the ship only knew the way to *England*, roughly ending up around the end of the 19$^{th}$ century/beginning of the 20$^{th}$ century each time they'd returned before. Yet here he was in Provo, Utah, USA, at the beginning of the 21$^{st}$ century. *Who would have guessed?* he thought to himself.

He turned his attention back to his exam. *This building is aptly named*, he thought as he stretched his toned arms and shifted in his seat. *"The Testing Center"*

Its real name was the Heber J. Grant building,

located on the south side of the Brigham Young University (BYU) campus, where Peter was attending school.

*Alright, you nasty little exam. You're just my next
adventure, and I WILL conquer you.*

Peter was all-in for adventures. And that's how he
framed things in his mind when they became challenging (or boring): 'the next adventure.' Though some
adventures, he admitted to himself, he would gladly
live without. Like exams. Oh well. At least he had something to look forward to once he finished. Wendy
always brought him fudge.

*I wish I could still fly when thinking happy thoughts.
Can't do that here, can I?* he mused as he looked around
the room. Fudge was a happy thought indeed.

He kinked his neck from side to side, extended his
legs out in front of him, and tackled his next adventure.
The anticipated fudge acted like a carrot hanging from
a stick to keep him motivated.

WENDY WAITED for Peter at their designated spot – the
lobby of the Harris Fine Arts Center, located at the
center of the BYU campus – for their monthly
rendezvous. At least, *she* liked to think of it as a
rendezvous since that sounded more romantic. Her
childhood crush on Peter still held in her mid-20s. She
knew that for Peter, their 'hanging out' as he called it,
was likely just a good excuse to land a free snack. *One
way to a man's heart is through his stomach*, Wendy
reasoned. So, each month she bought him fudge, and
Peter would come. Though seldom on time.

Wendy glanced at her watch and realized she'd been waiting for him for nearly 45 minutes. Though she'd used the time well by studying for her Psychology test, the temptation to be irritated was still there. Peter was hardly *ever* on time. For anything or anyone. Even her.

*Aren't I worth being on time for?* she wondered as she played with the end of her ponytail and tapped her fingers on her blue jeans.

She looked up and saw Peter swaggering his way toward her through the entrance. Yes, swaggering. That was the best way to describe his stride of confidence. He wore a dark gray t-shirt that hugged his chest and showed his well-defined muscles, denim jeans that hugged his legs in all the right places, and a leather jacket ("Because it makes me look even cooler," he'd once said to Wendy). He smiled cockily when he spotted her. She sat up straighter, her smile brightening.

"And what sort of delicacy have you brought me today?" Peter asked, sliding next to her on a lobby bench.

"Rocky Road fudge – it was just made today," Wendy answered. She clapped her hands excitedly in front of her, eager to have him try something new. Her homeland English accent became more pronounced when she was excited about something. She shifted, lifting a small white box from her green canvas messenger bag that sat beside her on the bench. She turned back to him, holding the box in both hands, an enthusiastic smile on her face.

Peter's expression turned from eager to irritated. "It

has *nuts* in it?!" he whined. "Who puts that into perfectly good fudge?" He made a disgusted face and shook his head, his auburn hair sweeping his forehead and over his slightly pointed ears with the motion. He brought his angular features around to stare at Wendy with his green eyes, his face serious now. "Wendy, you *know* I don't like nuts!" He smacked his leg for emphasis.

As Peter often put up a protest to new things, his reaction didn't surprise Wendy, though it was exasperating. "Yes," she countered with patience, "but Rocky Road also has marshmallows, and I *know* you love those," she reasoned with a wink. She was trying to quell the frustration rising in her so she could keep her calm tactics of persuasion going.

The thought crossed her mind that whenever they were together there was always some kind of argument that surfaced. She didn't like that thought. She had hoped that by this point – both in their mid-20s (at least, that's what Peter's physical appearance indicated) – they'd be past petty disagreements, the sort they'd had in Neverland.

"Oh, *fine*," he conceded with a huff and a roll of his eyes. "I'll try some." He flopped his hand out, palm up, and Wendy gave him the box. "But please, remember the things I *like* next time you bring fudge. I look forward to this every month, you know."

"Our meeting together?" Wendy asked, spurring a fluttering in her midsection. Maybe progress was in sight after all.

"The fudge," Peter answered over a mouthful. Apparently having nuts in it wasn't as awful as he'd fussed about. Things usually weren't as awful as Peter fussed about.

Wendy sent him a scowl, her hope of progress dropping a few notches. Peter sat chewing for a moment before a look of realization hit his gorgeous face. Turning abruptly to Wendy he amended, "Oh! The fudge *and* our meeting together. *Of course,* I look forward to seeing you, Wendy!" He leaned back, arms crossed, and gave her a charming smile.

Wendy relaxed and her features softened as he edited his original answer. She smiled at him, the hope of progress rising again. She appreciated when he gave her his full attention, which happened rarely. His full attention was also tenuous.

His head swiveled to the left and his eyes pulled away from Wendy toward an attractive girl across the room. He flashed a dashing smile at the girl and then winked. The girl hid a flirtatious grin behind her hand as she strode past.

After a few moments of watching the retreating form of the girl, he turned back to Wendy.

She was not amused.

Her hope of progress plummeted. Would he never *grow up*? She was sitting *right there* next to him, and he was ogling *some other girl*? Would he never think of anyone but himself?

Wendy, her face now holding an indignant expression, voiced her thoughts.

She tilted her head back and groaned. "*Seriously,* Peter?" she said with irritation. Her head came forward again. "Staring and flirting with some other girl," she flung her hand outward, "when I'm *right* here?!" She hit the bench next to his leg with her palm. Peter flinched.

Her volume rose a bit as her comments gained heat. "Am I just some convenient friend of yours?" She tilted her head to the side, giving him a scrutinizing look. "Like we haven't known each other since my childhood; as though we haven't been through the *craziest* of things together; as though I'm just *some other girl* who ought to adore you, simply because you're attractive, smart, and confident," she swept her hand up and down to indicate all of him. "Is *that* how you see *me*?" She put her hand on her chest.

Wendy's breathing had become quick and shallow as her frustration and hurt grew. She took deep breaths to calm herself. Nothing good would come from shouting accusations at Peter. Though she *was* still accusing him, hoping he would own up to his rude behavior.

Peter regarded her for about three seconds. "So, you think I'm attractive, eh?" he waggled his eyebrows, grinning from ear to ear. He leaned back on his hands, crossed one ankle over his other knee, and waited for her answer.

She tilted her head up and squinted her eyes shut in frustration, exhaling a huff. Then she stood and picked up her bag, intent on leaving and being done with this ridiculous conversation – she didn't appreciate him mocking her. *What a childish thing to do.*

"Wendy! Calm down!" Peter laughed. He reached out and took hold of her slender arm. She paused, curiosity over what he had to say winning out over her righteous indignation. She sat back down next to Peter on the bench.

"I was only joking! You're right; you deserve better." Peter's face was theatrically contrite. He reached out to take her hand, bouncing it on his knee.

Wendy took another deep breath and closed her eyes. As she opened them, she intensified her glare, assessing his sincerity. She wanted to think the best of him, so she gave a quick nod in acceptance of his apology. *Wait – did he even say he was sorry?*

Oh well. She let out a slow breath, then her eyebrows shot up as she remembered something.

"Here – have a look at this." She pulled out a half sheet of paper from her bag. "I thought this might be fun to do together, you and I." She gestured between the two of them.

The top of the white flyer read "Fencing Lessons" in bold, black lettering.

Peter gave a look of disinterest. "Fencing lessons?" he said dubiously. "This is ridiculous – I already *know* how to use a sword." He let out an indulgent chuckle. "And I'm rather good at it, if I do say so myself," he said with a crooked grin.

Wendy smiled with pursed lips, amused at his response.

*Time for some persuasion.*

"Yes, but how long has it been since you've *wielded* a sword?" she challenged as she leaned forward and raised an eyebrow.

Peter scowled, making Wendy laugh, which seemed to soften Peter. "I enjoy it when you laugh, Wendy." He sighed and unfolded his arms. "It seems our conversations usually turn toward arguing lately, and it's good to have you laugh. Even if *I'm* the one under scrutiny," he said with a pout.

This elicited Wendy's raised eyebrow again. She knew he didn't like that eyebrow; it meant she thought he'd done something wrong.

Gesturing at the flyer, Peter asked, "Who's teaching the class?" Wendy could tell he was trying to change the subject. He held out his hand for the paper, which Wendy handed over. His eyes scanned the information until he reached the bottom. "Who is 'Evan Roberts'?" he asked disdainfully. He looked up at Wendy and handed the flyer back to her. "Do you know him?"

Wendy shook her head. "No, I just saw the flyer outside my dance class earlier this week. It sparked memories of our adventures in," here she dropped her voice to a whisper, "*Neverland,*" she finished. "I thought it would be fun to do together." She shrugged her shoulders.

Peter seemed to deliberate for a moment, a serious look on his face. He sat up straight and took up an expression of superiority. "Fencing and sword fighting today," he waxed philosophically, "is useless. It's for little boys who wish to pretend an adventure." He waved his hand as though swatting at a fly.

"Peter, *you* were a little boy pretending an adventure – with *sword fighting,*" Wendy countered, raising that challenging eyebrow again. "Are you scared you might be outdone by the instructor?" she asked with a mocking smile. She rested her elbows on her knees with her face in her hands, staring at him expectantly.

"*No...!*" he defended, sitting up straighter and

clenching his hands over the front of the bench seat. "I'm simply thinking...it might be embarrassing for, uh, the instructor!" Peter concluded triumphantly. He relaxed his posture and smiled in satisfaction.

"The instructor?" Wendy asked, her eyebrows coming together. She pulled her head up from her hands and tilted it to the side. "How would you being there be embarrassing for him?"

Peter sat up and placed a hand on his hip. "I'm better at sword fighting," Peter explained. "It would be embarrassing for him if one of his students was better at it than him." He seemed to think this was the end of their discussion. He started gathering his things.

Wendy smirked; she had him right where she wanted him. "*That* remains to be seen," she dared him, leaning closer.

Peter stopped what he was doing and looked at her, his dark auburn eyebrows touching. "Yes, it does," he said with a mischievous smile. Then he leaned back, declaring nonchalantly, "But if something better comes along, I might change my mind."

Her hopes of gaining momentum with Peter in a romantic relationship had been waning. Repeated experiences like the one she'd just had with him had been adding up over time, like dust in an old attic. She'd been trying to remove that dust for years, but to no avail. It shouldn't be this difficult to even just be *friends* with Peter.

But she would take what she could get. Wendy had (sort of) convinced Peter to take fencing lessons with her. For now.

But why, oh *why*, was it so difficult to get to that

point? Why were things so difficult with Peter? And why did she feel like a smaller person when she was around him?

Peter's attention was again pulled away as another attractive girl walked by. He stood, slung his backpack over his shoulder, and glanced briefly at Wendy. "Later!" he shouted as he trotted in pursuit of the other girl.

## 2

W endy had noticed how much her brothers had grown since coming back to the real world – both in stature and maturity. They were both in their early-20s and studying at BYU like Wendy. Though John and Michael were brothers, their appearance and mannerisms held many differences.

John was tall, lean, and dark-haired. He'd traded out his glasses for contacts when he'd discovered they were a thing. ("This is the greatest discovery ever!" he'd exclaimed when wearing them for the first time.) His blue eyes were noticeably brighter without the glasses. And though he was a good-looking man, he was too oblivious to notice. Truth be told, John was oblivious to many things. Enthusiastic, but oblivious.

Michael, only a year younger than John, was of average height, broad and strong, with honey-colored hair like his sister. His brown eyes were intelligent and discerning, though he was more soft-spoken than John.

He was handsome in his own way but was too humble to make a fuss about it.

The one certain similarity they shared was their love of their sister.

Wendy entered their shared apartment and found her brothers studying in the front room. She saw John straighten from his seat on the couch. He looked up as their apartment door closed behind her. "Wendy!" he cheered, raising his hands in the air. "Come sit with us; we were just finishing our studies for the day." He closed his architecture textbook while Michael put away his lecture printout on history.

Wendy slowly entered the room, lost in thought. She noticed John pause as he took in her troubled expression. "You look as though you're working out a complex math problem," he said.

Wendy looked up at John. "What*ever* possessed us to leave England?" she said in exasperation.

She entered the small but tidy apartment, dropping herself onto their gray second-hand couch, which sat perpendicular to the one her brothers were on. She leaned her head back to rest and stared at the ceiling for a moment. She breathed in deeply, then exhaled a huff.

Her brothers exchanged a glance. "Wendy, we chose to leave England to *heal*," John began. "Then we all chose to leave Neverland to *progress*. And now we're here," he patted the couch seat he sat on. "I thought we'd all come to terms with how things happened," he added matter-of-factly.

Michael nudged John and gave him a stern look, flicking his head toward Wendy. Wendy saw an expression cross John's face as if a lightbulb went off in his head. He stood and went to sit next to her. "But that doesn't mean we made a wrong choice in either situation." He patted her hand. "So much good has come of it. And we still have each other." He gestured to the three of them.

Michael joined in, looking at Wendy. "How would we know what we now know if we hadn't made the choices we made?"

Wendy took a moment to put that sentence together in her mind. She looked at each of her brothers, nodding in concession that they were both correct. She shifted so she was now deeper into the couch.

"You're both happy here, then?" she asked them genuinely

"Immensely!" John said emphatically, slapping the couch for emphasis.

Wendy smiled at John's enthusiasm; it was hard to resist.

She turned to her other brother, whose ways were milder than John's. "Michael?" she asked.

"Very happy," he responded with a suppressed smile.

He and John looked at each other, wide grins spreading across their faces.

Wendy sensed there was more to Michael's answer. "What is it?" she asked, giving a curious smile while lifting her face off her hand.

"We met these girls today..." Michael said and shrugged.

"These two girls!" John inserted, sweeping his hands up and to the side, nearly hitting Wendy. "Both

exotic and vibrant. The one had this spunk about her –
wow!" His body collapsed backward onto the couch.

Michael joined in the praise. "The other – such an
angel. Like a spark shone from the inside." He ran a
hand through his hair, smiling ridiculously.

"So, you enjoy it here because of...girls?" Wendy
was trying to understand what they were getting at
while teasing them at the same time. She pinched her
lips together to keep from giggling at how smitten her
brothers were.

"*No...!*" John defended with a scowl. His hands
clenched slightly, sitting in his lap. Though a moment
later he tilted his chin up, his expression softening.

*He's thinking of that girl again*, Wendy thought.

"What John means," Michael sobered with a quick
shake of his head, "is that we enjoy being here for more
reasons than just new faces." He leaned forward. "This
location, this time in history. Machinery and science,
Wendy! Man has been to the *moon*! The technology
here is the stuff of novels we read when we were children. And indoor plumbing—"

"Amen to that!" John inserted.

Michael smiled and continued. "And the ease of
transportation. The progress and enlightenment." He
splayed his hands in front of him. "Several reasons."

Wendy nodded as her gaze fell to the floor, her
expression contemplative. "Yes, there are many reasons
to be happy where we are." She lifted her head to look
at her brothers. Forcing a smile on her face, she leaned
forward and gathered her things to head to her room.

"Wendy." Michael straightened; his voice held

concern. She looked up to find his expression confused. "Are *you* happy here?"

"Yes. Yes, I'm happy here," she reassured him with a reluctant smile. "For all the reasons you explained. And I love studying at the University. Where we live is lovely. We've met some great people. And I have both of you." She lifted her hand and gestured to her brothers.

"What more could you wish for?" John exclaimed with a wink and a smile, standing and placing a hand on Michael's back.

Wendy held John's gaze a moment; his smile faltered. She looked down, then to the side, as if lost in thought.

"I wish Peter would grow up." She looked back at her brothers briefly before standing and heading to her room down the hall.

## 3

Evan Roberts shifted his stance under the weight of the large dresser he and his fellow coworker, Coby, were slowly carrying up a flight of stairs. He enjoyed physical labor. It was fulfilling to do hard work, and it gave him time to think and reflect.

He had created a good life during the years he'd been in the real world. The location and time they'd landed in were unexpected, but not undesirable. And he was thrilled to be able to take advantage of the opportunity for a new life.

Evan's goals to change were coming along well. He'd taken anger management classes to re-train his brain and keep his temper in check. As the former "Captain Hook," anger had been second nature to him, and he wanted to amend that.

He'd attended Alcoholics Anonymous to drum away his thirst for rum (and any other alcoholic beverage). Being drunk took away his inhibitions; he wanted that gone from his life, too.

He'd found an honest line of work, a clean place to live, and had made a few friends. He'd even been out on a few dates. It felt freeing to be living this new life, this clean start.

His mind wandered again to Wendy, wondering where she was and what she was doing with her life. If she was happy with Peter. Evan wanted her to be happy. He had admired her from a distance in Neverland.

*I suppose I'm admiring her from a distance here*, he thought.

"Watch this last step, Evan," Coby warned, his American voice strong and deep. "It's a little higher than the rest."

Some of the old houses in Utah had been around for over a century. The stairwells were often narrow (which made moving large furniture up or down them rather complicated). And the ceilings were lower than more modern homes. But they were cozy, and people enjoyed living in them. At least for a while. Updated townhomes and apartment structures were popping up everywhere. Which was why being in the moving business was a profitable occupation at present.

His side job of teaching fencing was profitable as well. Though that was for more diverting reasons than just to earn an income. Evan took pleasure in the sport. Not only was it an intense form of exercise (all his students were sheening with sweat by the end of class), but it served as a reminder of what he had left behind. Which reminded him of what he was heading toward and working for each day. A new life, becoming a new person, and having the gift of a second chance.

They had made it to the top of the staircase, moved down the hallway, and into the room where the dresser was to be deposited. Carefully, Evan and Coby lowered it to the ground. They exhaled as they stood. Evan stretched his arms overhead, then tilted his head side to side to loosen the strained muscles in his neck. Coby put his hands on his hips and twisted his torso from side to side; then he looked around and surveyed the room. "Was that the last piece of furniture?" he asked, his large hands wiping sweat from his forehead with a handkerchief.

"I believe so. Let's go take a break before bringing in the boxes," Evan said in his British accent, and pointed toward the outside of the house.

They made their way down the stairs, ducking their heads to move their over 6-foot-tall bodies through the low front door.

Stepping into the sun, Evan wished his dark hair were lighter; the sunlight heated his head up faster than he would have liked. He also lamented having blue eyes, which were sensitive to daylight.

He shaded his eyes with one hand, the other having been severed from his body and fed to the infamous crocodile in Neverland. He twisted his lean torso from side to side, taking a moment to stretch again.

As Coby exited the house, he also shaded his eyes to block some of the sunshine. Evan went to the front cab of the moving van, pulling out a couple drinks and some prepackaged snacks. Sitting on the curb in front of the house, they ate and drank in silence for a few minutes.

"You sure you won't join this next round of lessons?" Evan asked as he stared at the mature sycamore tree across the street. He'd been inviting Coby for several months to his fencing class. Each invite had been unsuccessful, but Evan continued to ask.

"No thanks, my friend. Brings back weird memories," Coby answered with a shake of his head.

"Shame. Seems as though you'd be right agile with a sword." Evan looked askance at his coworker.

Coby cocked his head to look over at Evan, his brown, curly hair hanging a bit over his eyes. He smiled confidently. "I'm wicked with a sword, dude. Played at it all the time as a kid. I'm not too sharp in the noggin," he tapped the side of his head, "but I was good at that. But I don't know about taking it up again. It's part of something I want to leave behind."

Evan nodded, looking at nothing in particular in front of him. After a moment he sat up straighter and said, "The sharpness of the blade may be crucial in a sword fight. But remember that the hilt is the strongest part of the sword."

Coby looked at Evan, mild confusion on his face. "What do you mean?"

"Character is like the hilt. Whether or not a person is 'sharp in the noggin,'" he tapped Coby's head, "our character is more important."

Coby's expression seemed to internalize that thought for a few moments. Then suddenly he asked, "Hey, I've been wondering how you function with just one hand? And how do you sword fight and stuff like that? Also, what happened to your hand?" Coby gestured to Evan's right arm. "Was it, like, a work-related accident or something?"

Evan chuckled at Coby's questions; they'd worked together for almost a year, but this was the first time Coby had asked. "No, not work-related," Evan said while lifting the stump where his right hand used to be. "More like a childish prank that went too far. The little cretin fed my hand to a predatory animal after he cut it off."

Evan scowled at the memory, fresh anger toward Peter Pan rising from his chest to his head. He hadn't entertained that memory in such a long time. He squinted his eyes shut, catching himself before the anger grew. Using one of the breathing techniques he'd learned, he was able to calm his heart rate down and be in control of his emotions again.

He sat for a few breaths longer, then stood. "Let's finish with these boxes. Maybe we can head home early if we work fast enough."

"I bet I can carry in more than you this time," Coby challenged with a mischievous smile as he stood.

"You're on," Evan pointed at Coby, accepting the challenge.

As Coby headed toward the back of the moving van he turned to say, "I have a friend who did something like that to someone. We all thought it was funny; we were just kids. Looking back, that was really wrong of him. Pretty gross, actually. I don't think he ever apologized." He shook his head and jumped up into the back to heft the boxes.

Evan made no response; he could tell Coby was lost in thought after that. It made him wonder, though, if seriously maiming someone was an acceptable prank here in the real world as it had been in Neverland. Maybe it was just a phase young boys went through – taking things too far when harming others? He shook his head, turning his attention to the boxes that had yet to be moved into the house. He could get more boxes than Coby if he focused.

# 4

N ot far north of the BYU campus lay a haven of outdoor recreational supplies, a business called Outdoors Unlimited. Though Peter would have loved to boast that he had started such a business, he couldn't. But he could boast of working there. Which he absolutely loved. An entire store chock-full of everything one would need for outdoor adventures. Hiking, rock climbing, rowing, rafting, camping, fishing, summer gear, winter gear – all available for rent, and in some cases, to purchase.

The only thing better than working at such a place was the discounted rate Peter enjoyed as an employee. (And the only thing better than *that* was when there were only the girls at work, and they let him take any gear for free over a weekend. All he had to do was turn on his irresistible charm and the ladies were like putty in his hands.)

This particular weekend was one of those instances where Peter took advantage of free gear. Spring in

Provo Canyon was a sight to behold. Between the steady Provo River – beginning to swell with mountain run-off water – and the scent of foliage waking up after the winter season, it was a perfect time for a camping excursion for John, Michael, Peter, and the friends formerly known as The Lost Boys.

They no longer went by their Neverland names of Tootles, Slightly, Nibs, and Curley. Being men and wanting to leave behind their boyhood Neverland identities, they took on common names of men.

Thomas (Tootles) was in law school in hopes he might one day become a judge.

Slater (Slightly) had always been keen on music and was thick into it at the University.

Nick (Nibs) had become adept at architecture and was currently interning at a local firm.

And what Coby (Curly) lacked in wit, he made up for in brawn and heart, and found his niche working for a lucrative moving company.

The men hiked one of the many trails to a camping spot in the canyon. Though spring in Utah could be chilly, it had its warmer days. This was one such day. (Though, to be fair, 60 degrees Fahrenheit could be considered warm to one person and very cold to another. But after a Utah winter, 60 degrees felt warm to this group.) After setting up camp near a clear-running stream, under a canopy of Quaking Aspen trees, the friends used what was left of the daylight to explore their surroundings.

Neverland and the Utah mountains were very different from each other, but that didn't mean one was more preferable than the other. Their camping area was just as exciting to explore as Neverland had been. They came across several small animals (which Peter threw rocks at); some white-tailed deer (which Peter ran toward, yelling and flailing his arms); and a red fox (which Peter stealthily followed for about half a mile before getting bored with it). Despite his look of manhood, Peter still had many childish tendencies (as many college-age men do).

As shadows began to pass over the flora, the men started a campfire and pulled out food for the evening. After a hearty dinner, their stomachs full and their spirits high on the mountain air, conversation picked up.

Peter was distracted by the surrounding area for most of what John was saying, though he caught the last bit.

"*Every single lecture...*" John thwacked his hand on his leg with each word. "My biology professor would come in with a large picture of some insect, and say to us, 'Aren't bugs voluptuous?!'" He made a disgusted face. "I mean really, who says that about a *bug*?"

"An entomologist," Michael contributed with a teasing grin.

John shook his head with a resigned smile. "Rightly so, Michael. But still, such a word for an insect!" His face contorted in disgust again.

"What's an entomologist?" Coby asked, his American accent strong. The men were used to hearing him ask clarifying questions. Coby was a little slow on the uptake, though none of the friends thought any less of him for it. He was the only one who'd taken on the American accent. He had adapted quickly to the culture. *Or rather, forgot quickly how to speak British*, Peter thought.

"An entomologist is a scientist who studies insects," Thomas clarified in his know-it-all voice. "So, it would stand to reason that John's biology professor felt so strongly about them as to use expressive terms in describing his feelings toward them, as they were his life's study." He nodded once, seemingly satisfied with his comprehensive explanation. Being in law school had made him rather verbose.

"Can we talk about something else?" Peter whined, tossing his head back in exasperation and clenching his hands on his thighs. "I hated Biology 101 and talking about it makes me agitated."

"How many times did you have to retake the class?" Slater asked innocently, looking at Peter. Though Slater's studies in music were his main focus at BYU, he'd found Biology fascinating enough to minor in it.

Peter scowled at Slater's innocent question. "None of your business," he said defensively with a wave of his hand.

"You should've taken Slater up on his offer to help you with that class, Peter," Coby interjected, nodding his head toward Slater. "He's a genius with that biology stuff."

Peter's expression softened a bit at Coby's advice; he really *should* have done that. Oh well, he'd finally passed the class...after having to retake it twice.

"Well, what do *you* want to talk about then, Peter?" Nick asked, irritation in his voice.

Peter's expression turned mischievous as he surveyed the group. He smiled cockily, leaning back against a large rock and putting his hands behind his head. "Pranks," he said.

"Pranks?" Michael asked in confusion.

"Honestly, Peter!" John said with a fling of his hands. "We're out here in this beautiful setting, we haven't seen each other in months, and you want to talk about *pranks*? As in, pranks we used to do in Neverland?" John asked exasperatedly. His response shouldn't have surprised Peter; he knew that John was of the impression that talking about Neverland was not as worthwhile as talking about the present or the future.

Peter cast an annoyed look at John. *"No...!"* he defended. "Though we truly had some laughs at the expense of Hook and his ridiculous lot who had the audacity to call themselves 'pirates,'" Peter reminisced, chuckling to himself. He stretched out his legs and crossed his ankles.

"Yes, but we've moved on from all that," Thomas said as though addressing a child. "It was right fun to reminisce about when we first got here, but..." he trailed off hesitantly.

"But what?" Peter demanded, shooting a challenging look at Thomas. He couldn't see the harm in talking about past pranks and laughing at the expense of Hook and his crew.

"But like Thomas said, we've all moved on from that, Peter," Coby said guilelessly as he shifted position in his seat. If it had come from any of the other friends, Peter would have taken offense. But said in the innocence that came from Coby, it only made Peter irritated.

Peter sat up and looked around the group. "You've

all 'moved on'?" he asked, using air quotes. "You all want to *forget Neverland*?" He couldn't fathom why any of them would want to forget.

"Not forget it, but just...not hang out in that train of thought over and over. And over. Like we used to," Michael offered, looking a little sheepish.

Peter pinched his mouth closed, his eyes squinted and eyebrows scrunched in irritation.

"Suit yourselves," he said, suddenly relaxing his facial expression as though it didn't bother him in the slightest (though it did, in fact, bother him quite a lot). "I wasn't referring to past pranks in *Neverland* anyway." Peter rolled his eyes as though the thought was child-ish. In reality, he loved talking about anything where he came out the strongest, smartest, or most heroic.

Slater rolled his eyes at Peter's declaration. "Fair enough, Peter," he huffed, putting his face in one hand. "Tell us what kind of pranks you meant to talk about." He flung his hand toward Peter, an indication for him to carry on.

Peter looked around the group again, trying to build suspense. "April 1$^{st}$ is coming up soon..." he said with raised eyebrows.

"What's that got to do with pranks?" Coby asked, a bewildered look on his face.

"In American culture, April 1$^{st}$ is referred to as 'April Fool's Day' – a day for pranks and mischief," Thomas clarified for Coby. "I believe Peter intends to plan some sort of epic prank on an unsuspecting individual." He gave a satisfied nod at his assessment.

Peter's intent had been deciphered by Thomas, and he didn't like it. It stole all the glory from his revelation, and Peter hated having any glory stolen from him. He sat there glowering at Thomas, who in turn looked surprised at Peter. "What? What'd I do?" Thomas asked, looking around at everyone else.

"You stole his thunder," Nick enlightened Thomas, rolling his eyes. "Remember that Peter has never liked it when any of us know more than he does. Even though we're *not* in Neverland anymore and have all *grown up*, and such pettiness ought to be behind us." He shot Peter a disapproving look.

Peter shot one back at him, then closed his eyes with raised eyebrows and huffed a sigh out through his nose. "It is, indeed, my aim to pull an epic prank on an unsuspecting individual, as Thomas so *helpfully* pointed out," he said sarcastically as he waved a hand toward Thomas. "However, how are any of you to know who that unsuspecting individual is?" He opened his eyes and his gaze roamed from person to person, a challenging look on his face.

"You mean to scare us with your stares, Peter?" Slater disputed with an incredulous look. He sat up straighter and pointed his finger at Peter. "If some prank is played on us in the next few days, now we'll know exactly who to get back at. You've shown us all your cards; we've already caught you *red-handed*!"

At the mention of "red-handed," Coby's expression brightened. "Hey!" he clapped his hands in a single loud *smack*. "Remember that time Wendy pretended to be a pirate named Red-Handed Jill?" Coby may not have intended to disperse the tension among the group, but his comment had that effect all the same.

"Ha! I'd forgotten all about that. That was a right good prank of hers," Nick said, chuckling.

"I thought we weren't talking of pranks from Neverland," Peter griped with a look of incredulity. He tossed his hands up in irritation. He couldn't believe they had all come down on him for the idea of such a conversation, and here it was okay for someone else to bring it up. *Bunch of hypocrites*, he thought.

"Hey John, Michael – how is Wendy?" Thomas asked at the mention of their sister, looking over at the brothers. "It's been a while since we've seen her. I imagine she must have caught the attention of some bloke by now." He waggled his eyebrows. "Or is she perhaps still unattached? Is she still studying psychology? Has that ever made you feel under scrutiny living with someone who studies human behavior? I believe I would feel quite under the microscope," he chuckled nervously, "wondering if they were trying to analyze my every move, comment, action, what I ate, what I –"

"We get it, Thomas!" Peter interrupted, stomping the ground with one foot. He was tired of hearing Thomas go off about some silly thought like that. Wendy wasn't like that at all; she would never scrutinize Peter. Or would she? And the idea about her dating someone...

"Hang on!" Peter said, flinging his gaze to John and Michael. "*Is* she seeing someone exclusively? I didn't get that impression when I saw her last. She still seems quite taken with me – as most girls do," Peter concluded with a self-satisfied grin.

John and Michael stared at Peter for a moment,

seeming uncomfortable with Peter's assessment of their sister's interest in him.

John looked over to Thomas. "To answer your questions, Thomas – Wendy is doing well." John smiled. "She enjoys her studies, but never tries to psychoanalyze Michael or me, thankfully." He said this with a wink at Michael, who gave a half-smile back. "She works as a teacher's aid to the top Psychology professor. You know how she loves helping people; she's always had such a way with assisting others," he said with brotherly affection. "And as far as how her, uh, social life is going," John began tentatively, "she's not seeing anyone exclusively right now."

Silence hung in the air for a few breaths.

"Though she has been on several dates with different fellows," Michael contributed, looking up at John as though he'd forgotten that detail.

Peter frowned at Michael's comment. He didn't like that thought – the thought of *his* Wendy going out with other men. Wasn't he the only object of affection in her life? Not that they'd ever said that, in so many words.

Or at all, really.

But wasn't it some sort of unspoken understanding between them? He'd been the one to help them after her parents' death; he'd been the one to take her on adventures; he'd been the one to save her from Hook and his miscreants over and over in Neverland. Didn't she owe him her admiration and commitment? Didn't she owe it to him to not go looking around at other men – and especially to not go around dating them?

"You look confused, Peter," Coby voiced with his chin tilted down in concern. "You okay?"

Peter pasted a smile on his face and straightened his posture. "Of course! I'm fine! Never better," he lied. He couldn't voice his true thoughts aloud without the others rebuking him on Wendy's behalf. They just didn't understand her like he did. Even though he himself had gone around looking at other girls, dating them and flirting with them. But Peter didn't owe Wendy what she owed him, right? He was completely justified in his reasoning. Yes, he consoled himself – completely justified. The rules were different for him.

"Well," Thomas said. "It's getting quite late in the evening. Or early in the morning, depending on how you look at it," he chuckled at his joke. "Must be time to 'hit the hay,' as they say here. I, for one, ought to go to sleep soon. I have quite a lot of things to study tomorrow—"

"Alright, Thomas, we get it!" Peter interrupted again. Peter's agitation was tangible enough that everyone began to get into tents and sleeping bags without comment.

Except for Coby, who was oblivious to the tension. "Night, guys."

"Night, Coby," their voices carried in unison.

PETER LAY in his tent by himself. He preferred solitude when sleeping, even when they were in Neverland. He stewed in his thoughts – thoughts that irritated him. Like how the others had stressed the fact that they had all grown up and moved on.

Peter had grown up – he'd grown up quite nicely, if

the reactions of the opposite gender had anything to say about it. Which they did, he thought and smiled smugly. He felt he'd grown up better-looking than any of them in his group. And stronger, too. He kept up with being physically active. Thomas was becoming soft as a ball of dough in law school. The thought gave Peter a sense of triumph.

As his musings turned to Wendy, his sense of triumph wilted. He hadn't retained his position on her pedestal of importance like he thought he should. He needed to correct that. Or chasten her for it. He smiled roguishly at that thought. Yes, he would teach her a lesson. He would teach her that he was still the only hero in her life.

And he would teach her with a prank. She would be the unsuspecting individual who would be the brunt of his April Fool's prank. He extended his hands behind his head and closed his eyes, his lips widening in an impish grin. *I'll show her.*

## 5

Wendy straightened the stack of papers at her desk, relieved to be finished grading exams for her professor. He had given them to the students the previous week to allow plenty of time to finish. Now they could focus on the rest of their semester; finals would be coming up soon enough. Wendy and the rest of the students certainly appreciated it. She leaned back in her chair, tilting her head toward the ceiling with her eyes closed. She let out a sigh, satisfied with the day's work.

"All finished there, Wendy?" Professor Brown asked cheerfully. He was the head of the Psychology department at BYU. Wendy had worked as his teacher's aide for a few semesters. He was good to work for – flexible in his approach to her schedule, and always showing gratitude for her efforts.

Wendy startled, then straightened in her chair and gathered up the stack of papers. "All done, Professor," she said smiling, and handed them to him. He collected the papers, holding them against his chest with one arm.

"Thank you! You always finish grading these faster than me," he observed with a lighthearted chuckle. "Any plans for your weekend? It's certainly beautiful outside," Professor Brown said, tucking his free hand into his pocket.

"Plans..." Wendy began. She looked down at the desk and drummed her fingers on it, her expression a little lost. Her head had been swimming with psychology material for several hours and it took a moment to re-enter the present.

"Oh! Yes." She looked back up and flattened her palm on the desk. "But nothing that's outdoors, unfortunately. Though to get home I *will* need to walk." She tilted her head thoughtfully. "So I guess I'll enjoy being outside then. I'm actually starting a fencing class this evening. I'm a bit nervous, but quite excited about it." Her heart sped up with anticipation; it had been so long since she'd held anything remotely like a sword and she was eager to get at it again.

"Fencing!" Professor Brown's gray eyebrows shot up and his smile expanded. "Now that's not something we see often these days. Unless you're with the Medieval Club, or something like that," he mused, still smiling. "What got you interested in fencing?"

"Oh, there was an advertisement for it on campus. I thought it sounded interesting," Wendy said. She tucked a stray hair behind her ear. "I actually used to do a bit of swordplay when I was younger. It's been a while, though."

"That sounds well-rounded, if you ask me,"

Professor Brown said, nodding his head. His face turned contemplative. "Maybe I should take one of those physical activity classes at the Rec Center. I think they give discounts for senior citizens," he continued. "They've got Water Polo, Basketball, Racquetball, Jogging... Though jogging hurts my knees. Maybe not jogging." He shook his head and looked at the floor.

His rambling amused Wendy. She pressed her lips together to keep from laughing. The professor seemed lost in thought for a few moments, and the lull in conversation was quiet enough to hear the "tick-tock" of the wall clock.

"Tick-tock" reminded her of the infamous crocodile in Neverland. And the thought of the crocodile turned her thoughts to Captain Hook, who was usually on the lookout for the large, ugly beast who wanted to finish eating him.

*'Finish,' because Peter already gave that monster a taste of Hook when he fed his hand to it. Disturbing behavior,* she thought.

"Well, what are you waiting for?" Professor Brown broke Wendy from her rumination. "Go get your weekend started!" he said, nodding his head toward the office door and shooing her away with his free hand.

"Yes, sir!" Wendy said in mock-solute. She stood and collected her messenger bag. "Have a pleasant weekend with Mrs. Brown. And give those grandbabies a kiss for me when you see them," Wendy called over her shoulder as she headed for the door.

"I will," the professor promised.

～

WENDY, John, and Michael shared an apartment in a neighborhood south of campus. For any student to exit via the south part of campus, one must descend a very long hill. The hill had stairs for the ambitious, and a ramp for bikes, wheelchairs, and anyone else who truly wished to avoid the stairs. The walk was a pleasant one – plenty of trees for shade, bushes and flowers (depending on the season), and a small stream running along one part of the hill.

As lovely as the trek up or down the hill could be, it was best done during daylight hours when one could see what was around them. Though there were a few street lamps placed periodically on the hill to light the way, they provided little light at night. In fact, the effect was downright eerie with their greenish-yellowish glow. The trees and bushes and shadows suddenly became perfect hiding places for anyone wishing to ambush solitary pedestrians. Over time and with several attacks, the area had gained the moniker "Rape Hill." Most people using the hill at night were often seen in groups or traveling as quickly as possible to get to the top or bottom where it felt safer.

Wendy was very conscientious to ascend or descend the hill while it was light outside. Professor Brown had always sent her home before dark, and she was studious to check the time when not working in his office.

Today she savored the sunlight and warm spring weather on her walk down the hill toward home. The blossoms on the trees were beginning to bloom – pink and white petals with tiny green leaves. The bushes boasted a green hue as they woke from the winter season. Birds chirped and sang in the background. The air smelled new and fresh. Wendy tilted her head up to look at the trees, taking a deep breath of the spring scent. Her footfalls down the ramp made a steady beat, which reminded her of the tick-tock she'd heard earlier, which reminded her of the crocodile. Which brought her thoughts back to the dashing Captain Hook.

*What sort of thing does a villain do without a hero to contend with?* she wondered.

Since Peter had left Neverland, would Hook's life be free from disturbance? No more of Peter's shenanigans to pester the pirates; no more Peter playing the hero; no more ambushing Hook. Peter had saved Wendy from plenty of Hook's retaliations against Peter's pranks. Maybe the pirates could finally sail away by sea from Neverland and live out their lives in peace. *Is it possible to sail away from Neverland? Is Hook just as vengeful and tempestuous as ever?*

She'd begun to feel some sympathy for Hook before they left Neverland for the real world. Peter could be genuinely provoking, and Hook had been his favorite target. Ever since she'd grown up, Wendy had started to see how childish Peter's intrigues with the pirates had been. *Why couldn't he just leave them alone?* she had wondered. *What was there to prove? What had Captain Hook done to make Peter harass him so much?*

Truth be told, Wendy had always found the Captain rather attractive. He'd been several years older than her on her first visit to Neverland. But when she and her brothers returned after their parents' death, time in the real world had caught her up to his physical age. She remembered she'd felt herself blush in his presence the first time they encountered the pirates after their return. Her mature self could appreciate what her child self hadn't before. Deep blue eyes, dark hair, tall stature, chiseled form, a commanding presence, and a maturity that Peter had lacked. (That Peter *still* lacked.) Her heart rate had increased in Hook's presence and being captured by him in his attempts to lure Peter to danger had begun to feel exhilarating.

She shook her head at the memories. Hook was a villain; he had always been the villain. And he was in her past. Peter was in the present. And Peter was the hero. Sort of. *Maybe?*

But what kind of hero treated Wendy the way Peter treated her? Like some chum or convenient sidekick. Like she was supposed to sit on the shelf and wait for him to pull her down to admire him when he needed a boost to his ego. His ogling those girls during their last rendezvous hadn't been the first time Peter had ignored Wendy in favor of staring at a pretty girl in his line of sight. That didn't seem very gentlemanly. Or heroic.

Her musings carried her all the way home, where she deposited her messenger bag next to the coat rack near the front door. She expected to see John and Michael in the front room, where she usually found them either studying or playing video games. ("It's a brain break!" John often justified.)

Her brows knit in confusion as she took in the empty room and quiet apartment. "Oh! That's right," she said aloud with a jolt of recall, pointing her finger at nothing in particular. "Camping trip." She likely wouldn't see them until tomorrow afternoon, which meant she had the place to herself.

"Which means," she voiced while wagging her finger, "that I can listen to whatever music I want. As loud as I like." Her smile widened as she bounced on her toes and wiggled her fingers in anticipation. She glanced at her watch, wondering how much time she had to indulge in her choice of music until she needed to leave for the fencing class.

Concluding that there was at least enough time for half a dozen songs, she trotted over to the CD player, selected her favorite "Wendy's Mix" CD (which consisted of a blend of past and contemporary songs), hit Play, and cranked the volume up. She moved to the beat of the song "Breathless" by The Corrs while heading down the hallway to her room to get ready for class. Changing into something suitable for physical activity, she sang loudly off-key as the chorus of the song played.

## 6

W ithin walking distance to where Wendy, John, and Michael lived was a martial arts studio. It boasted several genres of classes – martial arts, yoga, Pilates, self-defense, and fencing. As she approached the building, Wendy wondered why she'd never thought to sign up for one of the classes before. Shrugging to herself, she entered and looked around for a place to put her bag. She found a pile of purses and backpacks lined up next to the wall mirror across the room.

It wasn't yet time for class to start, so she looked around for a place to sit while waiting. There were a handful of young men scattered around the perimeter of the room – some listening to music on headphones, and the rest checking out the cluster of girls sitting on the other side of the room. Wendy almost wished she could join them, but she had never quite fit in with other groups of girls – either in England in the past, or in America during the present.

So, she settled herself a few feet away from a young man with headphones on. The back of his head leaned against the window. His eyes were closed and one foot tapped out the beat to whatever song was playing.

*No need for awkward conversation if he's already occupied*, she thought with relief.

Her relief was short-lived. The young man opened one eye a moment after Wendy sat down. Then both eyes were open, his head turned toward her, and he pulled the headphones off his head. "Hey, I'm Dave," he greeted with a friendly smile, his dark hand outstretched. Wendy reached out and shook his hand.

"Wendy," she introduced herself, smiling shyly.

Dave's smile brightened, his teeth a stark white contrast to his brown skin. "This your first time?" he asked conversationally, stowing his headphones away.

"Yes – I saw an advertisement on campus and thought I'd give it a try," Wendy answered, shrugging her shoulders.

"My first time with fencing, too," Dave said. "I've taken martial arts here, and when I saw the flyer for the class on the bulletin board, I couldn't pass it up. I mean, girls think sword fighting is cool, right?" he asked, leaning a bit closer conspiratorially. "Girls want guys with skills, and all that."

He motioned his hand to the group of girls across the room. Most of them wore exercise jackets and matching pants, with glittering stripes down the side of the pant legs, their hair done up in two side-buns, looking almost like panda ears atop their heads.

*Fashion trends are an odd thing*, Wendy thought.

She pinched her lips to keep from laughing, except

it didn't work. A small giggle escaped, along with a smile. Dave's reasoning for being in the class was endearing rather than off-putting. He seemed to be a good-natured sort of person.

She continued the conversation with her hand out and palm up in explanation. "Martial arts seem enough of a skill to impress a girl, especially if used to defend her from some nefarious situation," she said in a mock-serious tone.

"I like your accent; it's fun," Dave said as he leaned his arms over the front of his legs. "The instructor has a British accent, too." He nodded toward the back office. "Do you do martial arts or anything like that?"

"I learned some self-defense at a church gathering once," she responded. She looked up in thought. "I've taken dance classes at BYU, and I actually used to do some sword fighting when I was younger," she said, shifting her position to face Dave. "It's been a long time; I wonder how much of it I remember?" She shook her head at her own question.

"Maybe it's like riding a bike?" Dave mused, his expression turning thoughtful. "Like muscle memory stuff – how it comes back to you after a bit of practice."

Wendy nodded in agreement, pulling her knees to her chest and wrapping her arms around her legs. "If that's the case," she began to tease, leaning her head forward, "are you ready to be beaten by a girl?" she finished with a raised eyebrow and a smirk. She'd only just met Dave, but she could already tell that a friendship between them was inevitable.

Dave lowered his voice in a mock whisper. "Only if you promise to not let me lose *too* badly," he smiled. "I don't want to look wimpy to any of those other girls sitting over there," he nodded toward the gaggle of girls.

"I promise," Wendy said, then laughed as she raised her right hand.

She seriously doubted that her skills with a sword would come back quickly. It had been several years since she'd even seen one, let alone used one. She, her brothers, Peter, and the Lost Boys had wielded swords so many times – playing with each other, fighting the pirates, battling other dangers. But they'd been gone from Neverland for a few years. Would she get the hang of it again?

"Can't wait for you to meet the instructor. This guy is *amazing*!" Dave exclaimed.

"You've met him before?" Wendy asked, still facing Dave.

"Evan Roberts? No, not personally. But I've seen him duke it out with other guys after my martial arts classes. Ching! Ching! Swish!" Dave pretended to wave a sword in front of him. Wendy smiled at his antics.

Dave's focus turned to the front of the room where the instructor stood to call the class to attention. Wendy took a moment to put her things aside, her focus on her bag.

"Welcome to Fencing. My name is Evan," he said.

Wendy's head perked up; she'd heard that voice before.

"We will begin today by practicing a few basics and becoming familiar with fencing terms," the instructor continued. "Have any of you ever used..." he stopped talking. Wendy finally looked up at the instructor, only to find him staring at her.

He was dressed in a dark grey, form-fitting cap-sleeve tank top and long black athletic pants. His dark hair was tied back in a low ponytail. He had deep blue eyes; a tall, lean form; a commanding presence; and his right hand was missing. He looked exactly like... "Hook," Wendy said breathlessly with widened eyes as her pulse quickened.

Dave swatted her arm lightly. "Dude!" he whispered loudly. "Just because he's missing a hand doesn't mean you gotta be snarky about it!"

She gave no reply to Dave. She just sat there, her heart in her throat and her pulse hammering, trying to figure out how and why Captain Hook was here in the real world.

EVAN HAD BEGUN TALKING to the class, looking around the room at the students. When he saw the girl sitting next to the window, he stopped. She had long honey-colored hair, delicate facial features, lovely blue eyes, and a regal stature (even while sitting). When she looked up at him, he knew for certain who she was. He heard her say "Hook." Intelligent thought left his brain, and all he could think of to say was, "Wendy?"

"You said you didn't know him!" the young man sitting next to her whispered loudly. Wendy glanced at her companion briefly before looking back at Evan. Her slack-jaw expression likely mirrored his own. What was she doing here? Not that he was *unhappy* to see her. But he'd never thought he would see her here. Or at all.

"Um," he said lamely, then gave his head a shake. "Have any of you ever used a sword?" He finally remembered where he was and what he was supposed to be doing. He was still staring at Wendy. All was quiet in the studio, and in the silence he could hear whispered comments coming from a group of girls near one side of the room.

"Why is he staring at her?"

"I don't know, she doesn't look all that hot to me."

"Do you think they know each other?"

Wendy tentatively raised her hand in answer to Evan's question. "I've used a sword before. Sir."

He smirked; of course she'd used a sword before. He'd seen her in action plenty of times to know how good she was with one. And how good she looked while using one.

*Focus, Roberts!* he told himself, though his heart rate increased at that thought.

She cocked her head and raised her eyebrow in response to his smirk. "But it's been...a while since I've used one." She narrowed her eyes at him.

"Well then, Miss Wendy, please step forward and let us see how much you remember," Evan said with a wicked grin, crooking his finger in invitation.

He went to the far side of the room, picked up two fencing foils with his left hand, and strode back to the front of the room. He looked at the girls gathered near the side. "Ladies," he addressed them. "As we will require additional space, I must ask you to proceed to the perimeter of the room, where you may remain unharmed." He gestured for them to move away. The girls smiled flirtatiously and did as he asked.

Wendy stood and walked toward him, her chin lifted. Evan tossed her one of the foils and she caught it while still looking at him. Her eyes widened; she seemed surprised she had caught it. They stood for a moment facing each other, sizing one another up.

Evan moved into position, foil pointed toward Wendy, his heart rate in high gear. "En garde, Miss Wendy," Evan said with a mischievous smile. *This should be fun.*

## 7

W endy was sweating by the time class ended. All the students were. Though her perspiration had come from more than just physical activity. Simply being around Hook had sent her pulse pounding through the roof.

*I should've brought a water bottle with me*, she thought. *A water bottle?!* Was that all she could think of after sparring with Hook? And his name – it wasn't Hook, or Captain Hook. *Of course not, you ninny! Why would he go by that name in the real world?* She shook her head once in frustration. This was *not* how she had expected the class to go.

"Dude, Wendy!" Dave came over, slapping his hand on her shoulder. "That was *awesome*! You've got *skills*!"

She smiled at his enthusiasm, temporarily forgetting her jumbled thoughts and emotions.

"You weren't so bad yourself for it being your first day," she answered, lightly punching him on the shoulder.

He smiled big. "Beginner's luck," he said modestly. He glanced quickly at his watch. "I gotta go, but I'll see you next week!" he said as he trotted toward the door.

"Bye!" Wendy waved. Her skills had come back to her faster than she thought. "Muscle memory" as Dave had called it, must be a real thing. It felt good to be using those muscles again though she could tell that she'd be sore by tomorrow. She reached her hands behind her back, stretching her arms.

The group of girls Dave had gestured toward at the beginning of class (whom he had dubbed "The Spice Girls Club") walked past Wendy as she moved into another stretch. ("Spicy what?!" Wendy had asked when Dave first called them that.) They each sent her scowling glares on their way out the door.

Wendy waited to roll her eyes until they had all left. *No wonder Dave calls them Spicy*, she thought. She continued stretching; it felt so good to help her muscles like that. *I should really start doing this at home.*

She'd been so wrapped up in stretching that she hadn't noticed all the other students had left. She bent down to pick up her bag, then sensed someone behind her. She stood, took a deep inhale, and let it out slowly as she turned around. She was staring at a man's tight chest in a dark grey shirt and had to tilt her head up to see the face that went with it.

"Miss Darling," Hook/Evan said with a polite nod, hand and stub on his hips.

*Did the heater kick on? It's suddenly too warm in here.*

"Sir," she responded as she stared into his eyes. They'd resorted to what they'd called each other in Neverland. "Or, Evan. Is that what you call yourself here?" she said, giving him a challenging look. She crossed her arms over her chest and felt her pulse continue to increase at his nearness. *Traitorous heart rate.*

"That's always been my name, Miss Darling," he said with a shake of his head. "It's who I was before 'Captain Hook'" (he used air quotes with his left hand), "and it's who I am now that I'm here."

Wendy narrowed her eyes in confusion. "It's always been your name? Why were you called Hook in," here she dropped her voice to a whisper, "Neverland?"

He smiled when she whispered the word. It was unnecessary, as they were the only ones in the building. "I never gave myself that name, Miss Darling—"

"It's just 'Wendy,' if you please," she waved her hand to get the formality out of the way.

"Very well then, Just Wendy," Evan smirked. Wendy scowled at his teasing but was pursing her lips to keep from smiling. "If you please, call me Evan. I was dubbed 'Captain Hook' by Peter after he...disposed of my hand." He lifted his right arm. "I put a hook there to replace what he'd taken." He waved his arm slightly before dropping it back down to his side.

Wendy had just been thinking of what Peter had done to Hook's hand – or, Evan's hand. Realizing that this man before her was more than just a pirate captain – that he had a real name – opened a curtain to a window in her mind that she hadn't known was there before.

But hold on, this man was a villain. Also –

"Wait – how did you get here?" Wendy asked in alarm, suddenly unfolding her arms and putting her hands on her hips. Evan opened his mouth to answer but Wendy quickly continued her interrogation before he could form any words.

"Did you follow us? Are you planning to harm us – to exact your revenge on Peter for good?" She tilted her head accusingly. "There's no magic here; he's as mortal as anyone in the real world."

She tapped her finger on her mouth and looked at the floor in consideration. "Yes, that must be it," she muttered to herself. "He must've followed us, knowing Peter would have no magic, couldn't fly away. Now he's here to–" She broke off from her rambling and looked back up at Evan, pointing an accusing finger at him. "Whatever it is you've come to do, just leave us all alone!"

She scowled and began to make for the door, but Evan had her by the arm before she made it two steps away. She turned and looked at his hand on her arm. Her skin tingled pleasantly where he touched her.

Then she looked at him. His facial expression held a pleading look, and he seemed hurt at her accusations. Wendy took a deep breath. *I haven't even given him a chance to answer my questions*, she thought. Her emotions faded from anger to contrition.

"I'm sorry for judging you so rashly," she said as she looked at the floor. Evan released his grip on her arm. "But given what you are, how can I not feel threatened by your presence here?" She looked back up and waved her hand to indicate the real world in general.

Evan crossed his arms over his solid chest. Wendy felt her neck heat up as she took in his chiseled arms.

He regarded her with a stern look for a few

moments. "And just what am I, Miss Darling?" he challenged, addressing her formally again.

"You're the villain. *Sir*." Wendy tilted her chin up defiantly, crossing her arms across her chest once more. She wouldn't be intimidated by him.

Evan gave a half-smile in response to her answer. Her heart suddenly felt like it was in her throat. *Ooh, that smile,* she thought. He'd used that particular smile in Neverland whenever he had the upper hand in a situation. And it had been just as disarming there as it was here. She felt light-headed for a moment and blinked her eyes several times, shaking her head to clear her thoughts.

Evan tilted his chin down and narrowed his eyes at her, still smiling. "Let me ask you something, Miss Darling," he said.

"Ask away, *Sir*," she challenged.

"Are you free this evening?" he asked, lifting his eyebrows.

"What?" Wendy said, completely thrown off guard. *What does that have to do with anything?* she wondered. She put her hands on her hips, jutting one hip out and cocking her head to the side.

"I thought we might take our conversation elsewhere," Evan said, mirroring her stance. "Unless you'd rather verbally spar in here," he looked around the room and then back at her.

Wendy stood straight, her expression serious. "I have no other plans tonight, but what makes you think I'd like to spend the time with you, *Sir*?"

He mimicked her stance again, a teasing smile tugging at his lips. "We can do away with the formalities, Wendy. We aren't in," here he leaned in and dramatically whispered, "Neverland," then back to normal volume, "anymore." He raised an eyebrow. "May I at least see you safely home?"

Wendy dropped one arm to hang by her side while jutting out her hip with the other hand on it. She cocked her head, feeling irritated. "I'm not going to show *you* where I live," she said fiercely.

He threw his head back and laughed at her irritation. *That laugh.* She shook her head again to get her thoughts centered. *Listen, head and body!* she thought. *Enough noticing things about this man that cause me to do anything other than distrust him. Especially noticing anything alluring about him!*

But that would be a difficult exercise in self-control. She dropped her head back to look at the ceiling, huffing out a breath.

When she looked back at Evan, all levity was gone from his face. He was staring at her exposed neck, then he looked her in the eyes. "May I at least answer your questions, and have you listen without judgment?" He looked down and to the side, rubbing the back of his neck briefly. He looked back up at her, waiting for an answer.

"Yes. I suppose we can do that," she conceded. She adjusted the strap of her bag on her shoulder and looked down.

He ducked his head to catch her attention. "Then let us be off."

～

WENDY WAS EXTREMELY fatigued from staying up late the night before, hearing Evan's story as they walked around a nearby park. Even when she *had* gone to bed, she couldn't fall asleep. Too many thoughts and questions kept her awake. She'd finally dozed off, only to wake up a few hours later unable to sleep anymore.

The morning came and went. She knew John and Michael would be home within the next couple hours. The day was beautiful again, so she decided to go for a slow walk to clear her head before her brothers came home.

*Do I tell them about Evan? Would they believe me? Yes, they would believe me. Would they believe his story? Is he really as reformed as he lets on? What about Peter – should he know about Hook? I mean, Evan? No, Peter would definitely do something rash and regrettable.*

At that thought, Wendy realized that Peter hadn't come to fencing class like he said he would. *More like he said he might,* she mused. He'd been out camping. *He probably forgot about it when he planned the campout,* she reasoned. He had seemed mildly interested in doing the class with her. *It's better that he didn't come,* she realized. *So, what now?*

Her stomach growled as she entered the apartment after her walk. She was hungry since she hadn't eaten breakfast. She popped a bowl of popcorn and sat in front of the television. Her mind was still so caught up in thoughts and questions that she didn't realize how out of character her actions were until her brothers arrived home.

She heard a key scratch at the doorknob, and a moment later the door swung open with John standing in the doorway. "We're ho-ome!" he sing-songed with a big grin. He and Michael began bringing in their bags and gear, setting them to the side of the door.

"How was your weekend, Wendy? We had a most interesting...time..." John cut off as he took in what Wendy was doing – sitting in front of the tv and eating popcorn. Michael looked up to see what had caught John off guard. His jaw went slack when he saw her.

"Wendy," John said with a hint of confusion in his voice, scratching his head. "Are you alright?" he asked, dropping what he was holding onto the floor. Michael approached Wendy slowly. He seemed shocked by her uncharacteristic behavior.

She looked up at her brothers, her mouth full of popcorn. She stopped chewing, swallowed, and looked down at the bowl. Then she looked at the tv, staring at it for several seconds. Then, glancing at the remote, she picked it up and turned off the tv. She stared forward before turning her gaze to John and Michael. She pasted a smile on her face to hide her embarrassment. "Welcome home!" she attempted with enthusiasm.

"Indeed," John said with eyebrows furrowed. It was obvious that he and Michael could tell something was off with their sister, but they seemed unsure how to broach the topic. "Uh, how was your weekend, Wendy?" John asked.

"Oh! It was..." she took a moment to find the right word. "Enlightening?" she said, testing to see if that answer would suffice. She looked from one brother to the other, feeling like she'd been caught with her hand in the cookie jar. How should she tell them?

She decided to skirt the topic for the present by

changing the subject. "How was the camping trip?" she waved to their gear and bags.

"It was fine," John answered, looking over at Michael, then back at Wendy. "Plenty to see and do up in the canyon. And it's always good to get together with the old gang. It did get a bit chilly during the night." Here he looked back at Michael, who merely shrugged as though the temperature hadn't bothered him. Silence hung for a few moments.

"Wendy," Michael hedged, "it's not like you to watch tv, and you hate popcorn." He scratched his head with a puzzled look on his face. "Could you tell us what's going on?"

Wendy looked from one brother to the other, then dropped her chin with a sigh. "Yes. Get yourselves settled first. There's a lot to tell and I'm not sure how to begin."

Her brothers washed up and put their things away. Michael made himself a bowl of popcorn (he was the only one of them who actually liked it) and dropped himself down on the couch. John came in from the kitchen holding a package of licorice in one hand, while the other hand held a piece up to his mouth.

Wendy surveyed what her brothers were eating. "Your snacks of choice," she said slowly, "are those typically chosen for more *entertaining* circumstances. Like going to the movies." She raised one eyebrow, questioning their motives in their food choices. "Do you think what I'm going to tell you will be *entertaining*?"

"*No...!*" John defended. "We just...feel like eating movie food. Right, Michael?" He looked to his brother for confirmation. Michael simply shrugged his shoulders and ate another handful of popcorn.

"Do I need to go get some soda?" Wendy teased, pointing toward the kitchen. John contemplated her question for a few seconds and had begun nodding his head before he seemed to realize she was joking. He smiled good-naturedly and said, "No, that won't be necessary. Carry on, Wendy! Tell us what's on your mind." He waved his hand to the side, still holding the floppy red licorice.

Wendy shifted around in her seat on the couch, then brought her knees up to her chest. She wrapped her arms around her legs, settling her chin on her knees. She took a fortifying breath before saying, "Remember how I was starting that fencing class?" she asked.

The brothers nodded in unison.

Her next question seemed to catch them off guard. "Remember how we thought we were the only ones to leave Neverland with Peter and the Boys?"

---

## 8

Peter came home from the camping trip feeling unsettled and upset. He didn't like that his friends hadn't been as keen on his company or his opinion as they had usually been. He'd always been the leader of the group, but since landing in the real world, they'd been coming into their own and depended less and less on his direction and approval. He took it as a personal insult.

*Maybe if they don't need me anymore, then I don't need them anymore. After all I've done for them, you'd think they'd still respect my position. They said they've grown up and are moving on. Well, they aren't growing up to be very respectful adults now, are they? Bunch of self-important, ungrateful "friends."*

He huffed and clenched his fists at his sides, looking around his room.

He didn't feel like putting his things away at the moment. Those could wait until later. He spied the camping gear he'd borrowed from work, then looked at the clock. He breathed a sigh of relief seeing that there was time to clean himself up before leaving for Outdoors Unlimited.

*Don't want to smell like a skunk around the ladies at work,* he thought with a grin. Unless he'd be working with some of the guys. But even then, he liked to impress others, and smelling bad wasn't impressive. *Besides, what if some lovely customer comes in this afternoon? Want to look my best.* He nodded his head in conclusion to his thoughts, then headed toward the bathroom to clean up.

He arrived a little late for work, but punctuality had never been his thing. His arms were full of camping gear, anyway. He hated making more than one trip to get anything from one place to another. He stored away the items in their respective places, then headed to the front desk to see who he was working with.

Outdoors Unlimited was always busy on the weekends. That day was no exception; there were people all around the store. His fellow employees that day consisted of 3 girls and 2 other guys. He kinked his head from side to side and headed out into the fray of customers.

Time flies quickly when one is busy, and such was the case for Peter that afternoon. The dinner hour rolled around, and the customers trickled out. The employees who weren't helping customers at the front of the store were in the backroom, stocking shelves with supplies during the lull. Peter looked around and realized he had the three girl employees to himself as they worked.

"And how has your weekend been, ladies?" he struck up a conversation flirtatiously.

The girls looked at him, smiling. Then they looked at each other as though to say "who wants to answer first?" A girl with tan skin and dark hair did. She giggled. "It was great! Some friends and I took a quick trip to Vegas for a few days! Just a fun impromptu girls' trip." She waved her hand like it was no big deal.

"Ooh!" a girl with blonde hair and blue eyes gushed. "Where did you stay? What did you guys do? I haven't been to Vegas in *forever!*" She stopped what she was doing and turned her full attention to the dark-haired girl. "Did you see any shows? Did you meet any guys?" she asked, lifting her eyebrows up and down.

The dark-haired girl sighed. "No guys," she frowned dramatically. "But we got to see *Stomp!* It was incredible!" She waved her hands excitedly back and forth in front of her.

"I've heard that's a must-see in Vegas!" the third girl exclaimed. "Did you eat at any cool places? And you didn't tell us where you stayed!" She placed a hand on her hip. At this point, no one was stocking shelves anymore.

"We stayed with a friend," the dark-haired girl shrugged. "I wish I could afford to stay at the casinos. But they're always so noisy and smell funny anyway." She scrunched her nose. "Oh! But we got to eat at this crazy awesome buffet called The Wicked Spoon! *So* cool!" She waved her hand emphatically. "They had these crepes and these giant pastries! I think I gained 10 pounds in that one meal," she giggled and put her hand on her midsection.

"From my vantage point," Peter interjected, "I find no flaws with your figure." He winked at her.

The dark-haired girl covered her mouth to hide her smile, though she pretended to be affronted. "Peter! You are *such* a flirt!" She put one hand on her hip and used the other hand to swat his shoulder. Peter grinned in satisfaction.

"Why do you all have to look so good?! I can't concentrate on what I'm doing!" He raised one eyebrow coyly and gave the girls his charming half-smile.

The girls looked at each other, giggling. The third girl rolled her eyes playfully. "You're just saying that!" she nudged him with her foot. "What did you do this weekend, Peter? I saw you take all that camping gear out last week," she said as she cocked her head to the side curiously.

Peter mimicked her, cocking his head to the side playfully and smiling at her. "You're adorable when you do that," he complimented. She smiled back.

"I went camping with some old friends," he answered, straightening. "Just a quick guys-trip. Nothing fancy. Though it wasn't as much fun as I had anticipated." He looked to the ground with a frown. "Seems my friends don't need me as much as they used to."

"Oh *Peter*! What happened?" the blonde girl asked compassionately, putting her hand on his arm. Peter felt a sense of triumph seeing he had gained someone's sympathy.

"I guess they've moved on from me," he said with a sad shake of his head. "Whenever I tried to contribute to the conversation someone would brush off my ideas and opinions." He splayed one hand on his chest. "Like I don't matter anymore."

"Awww!" the girls chorused in unison.

"That's a terrible feeling!" the third girl said. "They don't sound like good friends to me." The other girls nodded in agreement. "Maybe they're just jealous of you."

"Jealous? Of *me*?" Peter asked innocently with wide eyes, placing his other hand on his chest. "Whyever would anyone be jealous of me?" he asked, feigning modesty.

"Peter! *Look* at you!" the dark-haired girl exclaimed while gesturing with both hands at Peter. "You're smart, hard-working, you have a British accent, and you're *totally* hot!" She placed a hand on his shoulder. "What guy wouldn't be jealous of that? Maybe they feel threatened when you're around." The girls all nodded in unison.

Peter put his hand up to his chin, contemplating the idea. He was enjoying this immensely! He loved playing Attention Seeking Through Pity Party.

"Oh, that's gotta be it," the blonde said, shooting her finger out. "Guys feel threatened by each other *all* the time!" She waved a hand in front of her. "So, I ran into my ex-boyfriend once when I was on a date with this other guy. It was like watching a bunch of gorillas battle on Animal Planet, or something. The way they sized each other up and were, like, making veiled insults at each other. I think my date even tried to look taller, standing up straighter at one point." She lifted her hand, indicating increased height. The other girls shook their heads distastefully.

"That might be it." Peter pursed his lips in thought. "But what am I to do?" He shrugged with hands out to the side. "Where will I find friends? Especially if every guy out there is feeling intimidated by me?" He looked each girl in the eyes, willing them to respond the way he wanted them to.

"*Peter!*" the dark-haired girl said while dropping her hands to the side, as though the answer was obvious. "*We're* your friends!" She gestured to herself and the other girls, who nodded vigorously. "You can hang out with any of us *any*time! Right, ladies?" She looked to the other girls for backup. They were both still nodding in agreement.

"*Any*time," the third girl echoed.

"Like, totally," the blonde answered.

"I'm getting together with some other girlfriends tonight," the dark-haired girl said, nudging him with her shoulder flirtatiously. "You wanna come?"

Peter looked at each of them with pretend humble gratitude, though his ego was doing a victory dance at his successful manipulation of these girls' sympathies. He didn't need the Lost Boys or Wendy's brothers. He had better people to be around now.

"Thank you, ladies. You're truly good friends." He tilted his chin down demurely.

At that moment, the other two guy employees entered the room. "Where have you all been?" the first one asked in mild annoyance, placing his hand on the side of the doorway. "It's nearly time to close – we need help putting things away in the front." He scowled at Peter in accusation. The other guy folded his arms across his chest, straightening his posture and appearing taller.

The girls all looked at each other, then looked at Peter. "I rest my case," the blonde said, pointing at the guys and lifting her eyebrows triumphantly.

Peter slowly nodded his head, agreeing with her assessment. All three girls lifted their noses disdainfully and strode past the two guys without looking at them. When they were out of earshot the first guy asked, "What's up with them?" hooking his thumb in the direction of the girls. Peter merely shrugged his shoulders with his hands out to the side.

*Maybe this weekend won't turn out so bad after all*, he thought with satisfaction.

9

M onday morning came bright and early, and with it, a day's worth of moving jobs to tackle. Evan was checking the moving van to prepare for departure when Coby arrived.

"Hey Evan," Coby greeted. He walked over to where Evan stood at the back of the truck, making sure the lock on the sliding door was working.

"Coby – good morning," Evan responded, glancing back at his coworker. "I hope you had breakfast because there's a lot to move today. You'll need the energy."

"It's the most important meal of the day," Coby said, smiling at the old adage. "I wouldn't miss it." He headed over to the assignment desk to pick up their list, then headed back to the moving van.

Evan sat in the driver's seat, making sure all things were in order in the cab of the van. Coby swung up into the passenger seat and put the list on the dashboard. "Let's roll," he nodded forward.

Evan sat without starting the van and looked over at Coby. He raised his eyebrows, nodded his head at Coby's seatbelt, and said, "Aren't you forgetting something?"

"What?" Coby asked, bewildered. He looked around his seat, down at the floor, then out the window.

Evan chuckled. "Your seatbelt." He nodded to it again. "Not only will it keep you from flying from the vehicle in the event of an accident, but we could be fined if we get pulled over."

"So just drive the speed limit," Coby razzed as he buckled up. Evan started the engine and shook his head, smiling. "What'd you do this weekend?" Coby asked as they rolled out onto the street.

Evan's thoughts immediately went to Wendy. How they'd sparred at his class; the conversation afterward; her accusations of Evan having nefarious intentions; and the chance he had later to explain what he was doing there, how he'd gotten there, and his efforts to make something more of his life.

He must have been quiet for too long. "That bad, huh?" Coby prodded with caution.

"No, sorry." Evan gave his head a small shake. "It was an interesting weekend. I ran into...an old friend. We were able to catch up; it's been a few years."

"Was your friend at the class? How did that go?" Coby asked.

"Class went well." Evan took a deep breath and drew it out slowly. "And yes, my friend was there. We showed everyone a few fencing moves." He shifted in his seat, not yet comfortable talking about his interactions with Wendy. "What did you do this weekend,

Coby?" he asked, glancing over and changing the subject.

"Went camping with some old friends. Good times." He nodded his head and smiled. "Had some laughs, ate some food, slept in the cold. It gets *super* cold up the canyon at night! I wasn't in a tent."

"You mean you didn't *have* a tent, or you *chose* not to sleep in one?" Evan asked, looking quickly over at Coby.

"Oh, I chose not to. I like seeing the stars." He shrugged. "But if I do that again I'm bringing a beanie to keep my head warm." His body shuddered involuntarily. "It was *so* freaking cold."

"Hmm," Evan said, smirking. "Not just 'cold', but 'freaking cold.' That must be frigid, indeed."

Coby swatted Evan's side, then reached for the list of moving jobs for the day. "Is the first job an office move? This doesn't look like a house address," he asked with a scrutinous look on his face.

"Yes, just moving from one downtown office to another," Evan said. He tilted his head to the side. "It shouldn't take too long, and they're both on the ground floor."

"Nice," Coby said. He put his fist out and did a "pound it" with Evan. "What's after that?" He consulted the list. "Is that next address for the new apartment complex south of BYU? I wonder what it's like going to school there." He let the list fall to his lap and looked contemplatively out the front window.

Evan knew Wendy was studying at BYU, but that's all he knew. He wondered what she studied, and if her brothers were also students there – if Peter was a student there, and where Peter worked. He should've asked Wendy so he could avoid the place. He hoped he could ask her after fencing this week. If she came again. She'd given no indication otherwise. He wanted to see her again. His heart rate increased just thinking of her.

Coby and Evan made quick work of the first two jobs, enough so that they had time to stop for more than a quick snack break in the early afternoon. They ordered Subway sandwiches and ate in the moving van. Conversation started up as they finished eating.

Evan looked over at Coby. "Where are your friends from? Do they live around here?" Evan was curious about the campout – if anyone had traveled far to meet up with Coby.

"We all live around here," Coby answered with a shrug. "Well, here-ish." He tilted his head side to side. "One's in law school; one's studying music; one is interning at a company in Salt Lake; then there's two brothers, both at BYU; and the last one's at BYU too, but I'm not sure what he's doing with school. He keeps having to retake classes because he's kinda lazy." Coby smiled and shrugged. "I think he works at that outdoors supply place north of campus. That's where we get a lot of our camping gear. He gets to use it some-times. Nice of him to let us borrow it."

Coby paused in thought for a moment. "The brothers have a sister, but she didn't come. She usually doesn't. Not really her thing anymore. I wish I could take her out on a date, but we're all more like brothers to her. Except for the one guy who works at the outdoors place. I think she's had a thing for him for a while."

Coby paused again, then suddenly – "Hey! Maybe I could set *you* up with her!" His face lit up at the idea and he turned to face Evan.

Evan laughed uncomfortably. "I'm honored that you think I'd be a good choice for your friends' sister," he said. "I don't know, but I'll think about it," he added.

Coby regarded Evan for a few moments. "You're a good guy, Evan," he said. "You need a good girl."

The compliment was validating – Evan had been working for years to become a "good guy," as Coby put it. But he still wasn't comfortable being set up on a date.

"I thought you said she was interested in one of your other friends," Evan countered, lifting his eyebrows.

"Yeah, but he's been stringing her along forever. Like he can't decide if he wants to go for it, you know?" Coby faced front again and seemed lost in thought. Then his eyes widened. "I better watch my back this week. My friend hinted at some kind of prank for April Pools," he said, shaking his head. "I hate getting wet."

"Do you mean 'April Fools'?" Evan asked, hiding a grin.

Coby smiled good-naturedly. "Yeah, that. Anyway, the guy has pulled some *serious* pranks in the past! He doesn't really think before he acts. But then again, I don't really think before I talk." He squinted one eye as though that would help him puzzle it out.

Evan looked over at his friend. "You're a good sort, Coby. Give yourself some credit."

Coby nodded in agreement. "I know I'm a good guy. Just slower than most people, but I'm okay with it." He looked at the clock on the dashboard. "We better get going again. Where's the next place?"

That night after work, Evan thought back on his conversation with Coby. He hoped Coby wouldn't be the target of someone's prank; he was a genuinely good person and didn't need to be the brunt of a trick.

He also hoped Coby wouldn't bring up the idea of setting him up on a date again. Because now that he'd seen Wendy, he doubted any other girl could drive her from his mind. Or his emotions.

## 10

The city of Provo had a reputation for having a high population of the religious. There were quite a few members of The Church of Jesus Christ of Latter-day Saints that lived there and in the surrounding areas. Several chapels for the Church dotted the city, but even with so many chapels, there still wasn't room enough to send BYU students to a chapel for church meetings and activities. So, church services and activities were often held on the BYU campus, in classrooms and conference rooms.

Such was the case for the weekly Monday night activities that Wendy, John, and Michael attended. They themselves weren't members of that religion, but they enjoyed the opportunity to surround themselves with other young adults their age in an uplifting setting to socialize. ("And the desserts they serve afterward are worth it!" John had said more than once.)

The activity that night was a game called "Bigger and Better." The group of young adults split into teams, and each team started with a small object (like a penny, or a pencil, or maybe even a stick of gum). The purpose of the game was to go door to door, asking for something "bigger and better." At the end of the allotted time, the groups reconvened to compare who ended up with the biggest and the best object.

Wendy's group won the bragging rights after the game – someone had given them a *couch*. It took all of her teammates and someone's truck to get it back to the designated meeting spot. (They gave the couch back to the owners afterward.) The game was a silly one, but all in good fun, it being April 1$^{st}$ – a day for silly things.

After the game had ended, the refreshments had been eaten ("Donuts! Oh, I *love* donuts!" John had exclaimed), and the couch had been returned, the group began to disperse. Before Wendy and her brothers left, she spotted a friend who had loaned her a dress the month before.

"I need to go talk to Megan," Wendy said to her brothers, stopping and pointing to her friend. "Head home without me; I'll be there soon."

She smiled reassuringly at her brothers, who nodded and began walking home. It was still light outside – light enough to go down the notorious hill south of campus in safety. Satisfied that her brothers were on their way, Wendy headed toward her friend. "Megan!" she called.

Megan turned at the sound of her name. "Hey, Wendy! How's it going?" she greeted.

"I need to return that dress you loaned me!" Wendy laughed uncomfortably. "But I left it at home..."

"It's okay – I don't need it back anytime soon,"

Megan said. "But do you have any gum? I want to go talk to that new guy and I don't want stinky breath," she said, peeking into Wendy's bag.

"Yes, I do," Wendy answered, looking up at Megan and waggling her eyebrows.

"Where did it go?" she asked herself as she searched through her bag. "There it is!" Success lit her features. "But where's my wallet? Oh!" She snapped her fingers and pointed. "I must've left it at Professor Brown's office."

"I'm gonna go talk to that guy," Megan said, smiling with excitement.

"Good luck, Megan," Wendy said, winking. "I'll see you later."

Wendy began the trek across campus toward the professor's office. Once she arrived, she unlocked the door with her office key. After entering, she turned on the lights and went to her desk. Seeing no wallet on top of the desk, she opened one of the drawers. And there was her wallet, sitting next to a bag of chocolate.

"That's right," she thought out loud. "I went to the vending machine earlier today. Must've stuffed both of these in here when I got back." She immediately put her wallet in her bag, patting it safely after closing it.

She turned to leave and was startled when a student rushed into the room, huffing and puffing. The girl stopped and bent over, taking deep breaths. After her breathing had slowed, she held out something to Wendy. "Here," she said. "I know it's a day late, but Professor Brown said he'd still take it. It's my exam."

"Oh." Wendy reached out and took the papers from

the student. "I'll leave him a note to let him know you left it here tonight."

"Thanks! Okay, bye!" The girl turned and sprinted down the hallway.

Wendy smiled and shook her head. She looked down at the girl's exam. She had graded so many of these tests last week; what was one more? It would help the professor out, and he could submit the grades that much sooner. She hung her bag across the back of her desk chair and sat down to work.

Grading the test took longer than she had anticipated. The student had atrocious handwriting. Unfortunately, the daylight slipped away quicker than she thought. By the time Wendy sat up, it was dark outside. She looked at the clock, willing it to go backward and bring the sun back up again. Knowing that would be futile, she sighed in resignation, wondering if she should call John or Michael to come up and walk her home. *I don't want to bother them; I should be okay on my own*, she reasoned.

She set the exam on the professor's desk with a note explaining how the student had turned it in that evening. Spinning around in a circle to see if she'd forgotten anything, she spied her bag hanging from her chair. She strode over to it. "I'm not leaving without you," she muttered. She slung the bag strap across her body, flipped her hair out of the way, and walked to the door. Turning off the lights, she locked the office up and headed down the hall toward the exit.

It was darker outside than she thought. A layer of clouds blocked any moonlight there might have been. Periodic streetlamps lit the way down the sidewalk toward the south part of campus. She crossed the last street and stood at the open grass field that surrounded the sidewalk leading to the hill. Wendy gripped her bag strap, lifted her chin, and walked resolutely down the hill. She could hear voices in the distance – probably other students out doing their Monday night activities. The sounds of life nearby calmed her nerves, and she slowed her pace just a little.

*This isn't so bad. I'm the only one here; nothing to worry about.*

She changed her mind when she saw a masculine figure wearing a dark hoodie round the corner in front of her.

*There's nothing to be afraid of; he's just heading up to campus*, Wendy reassured herself. She kept walking with purpose, trying to convey the message "you don't want to mess with me."

But the stranger stopped walking and blocked her path. Panic seized her mind and rational thought fled. She stood frozen for a moment.

Wendy tried walking around him to the right; he shifted in front of her. Her panic rose and she tried to go left; he blocked her path again. *What do I do?* She sent a silent prayer heavenward.

Her mind cleared. She thought of an idea to improvise.

She went slack and fell to the ground as though she had fainted, accidentally landing first on her knees before toppling over. The impact on her knees was painful, but her tactic was that of distraction. The man took a few hesitant steps forward. He came and knelt down next to her, leaning forward toward her face.

As he lowered his head to see more closely, she waited until he was in range to push him in the chest with every bit of strength she had, huffing out a strong breath. He went flying backward, landing with a loud *thump* on his back. He grunted and groaned.

Wendy jumped up as quickly as her injured knees would let her. The figure stretched a hand toward her ankle, but Wendy pulled out of his reach. Then she hurried down the hill.

She tried running but her knees protested in sharp pain. She pushed past the pain as best she could and headed the rest of the way down the hill, holding the railing for stability. When she reached the bottom, where there was the safety of people and vehicles, she stopped to catch her breath. She had to sit down on the sidewalk; her knees wouldn't let her stand anymore.

She put her face in her hands as sobs began to shake her body. She didn't care that people could see her in distress; she was *glad* people were around. There was safety in numbers. She was in shock, and she cried for what felt like an hour.

Wendy flinched when she felt a hand on her shoulder. Her terror came back full force, thinking it was the hooded figure from the hill. She flung her hand out, trying to deflect whoever had touched her, but her wrist was caught by a strong grip. She looked up to see whose hand it was.

Relief flooded through her from her scalp down to her toes. It wasn't the hooded figure who had blocked her path. It was... "Peter!"

## 11

P eter carried Wendy into her apartment. She felt so safe in his arms. John and Michael were sitting on the couch, a phone held up to John's ear. "Never mind, Officer. She's here – we found her!" He hung up as he and Michael jumped up from the couch.

"Wendy! What on earth happened!" John exclaimed, thrusting his hands through his hair.

Peter put Wendy gently on the couch. *He's rather strong*, Wendy thought. *Maybe Peter is still a hero after all.*

Michael came over with a damp cloth and began wiping dirt from her arms and face. *I must look awful.* She looked up at Michael, who smiled reassuringly at her. "You're safe, Wendy. You're home," he said soothingly. She closed her eyes and tried to let her body relax.

She suddenly remembered who had brought her home. "Peter!" She sat up quickly from the couch.

John put a hand on her shoulder, encouraging her

to lay back down. "He's still here, Wendy. It's okay," John said.

Wendy looked to where Peter stood across the room, leaning against the wall with arms folded and watching her.

"I'm so glad you were there, Peter," she said.

He walked over to her. Michael stood, giving Peter space to kneel next to Wendy's prone figure on the couch. He smoothed her hair back. "Shh. John and Michael are right – you're safe. It's okay," he whispered.

She felt so much gratitude. *How would I have gotten home on my own? I can barely walk.*

"Michael," Peter addressed her brother. "Please get Wendy something to drink. Her mouth has probably gone dry from shock."

Michael obeyed immediately, coming back a moment later from the kitchen with a glass of water. Peter helped Wendy sit up enough to take a few sips. He handed the glass back to Michael and helped Wendy lay back down. He smoothed her hair back again, then looked up at her brothers.

"I need to head home, but make sure she gets plenty of rest. She'll heal quicker that way," Peter said. Both brothers nodded their heads vigorously. Peter stood from where he'd been kneeling next to Wendy.

"Thank you, Peter. You saved our sister," John said, putting his hand on Peter's shoulder.

Michael nodded his head in assent, patting Peter on the back. Peter winced at Michael's touch.

"Truly, Peter," Wendy said from the couch. All three men turned to look at her. "That was a very kind and heroic thing to do, helping me home." She smiled as best she could. Her head and body hurt from earlier, but she wanted to give Peter a smile to show her gratitude.

Peter waved his hand to the side. "It was nothing," he smiled back at her. "I'm glad I was there when I was." And with that, Peter bid them goodnight and left the apartment, closing the door behind him.

Right after the door was shut, John locked it. Turning back to Wendy, he said, "What happened?! Were you hit by a car?" He walked over to the couch and sat on the floor, Michael following right behind him. "We left the activity two and a half hours ago! What happened afterward?"

Wendy told how she'd needed to go back to Professor Brown's office to retrieve her wallet, and how she'd stayed longer than she anticipated grading the late test. She told them she'd thought about calling them to come walk her home but didn't want to bother them.

"Bother us?! Wendy, you're our sister – we would do *anything* for you!" John declared while waving his hand to the side, indicating the vast amount of whatever they would do for her.

"We wish you would've called us," Michael said from the floor. "But please, finish telling us what happened."

"I was headed down the hill–" she said.

"*Rape* Hill," John inserted with a scowl.

"Yes, John," she frowned at the interruption. "A man came around the corner when I was about halfway down. He kept blocking my path, so I pretended to faint and did some improvisation to get away."

She continued her narrative until it came full circle with Peter carrying her into the apartment. "I could hardly walk. I don't even know how I got down the rest of the hill. But Peter helped me hobble home, then carried me in. I'm so grateful he was there."

She closed her eyes and put her hand on her head, feeling strained from telling her story. "Could you boys help me to my room? I think I just want to sleep."

Michael assisted her off the couch and down the hall. He and John went to the kitchen, then came back with Ibuprofen, a glass of water, and some chocolate.

"Mother always said that chocolate helps you feel better," Michael offered.

Wendy took the medicine and chased it down with a piece of chocolate. "She was right," she said with a smile.

Her brothers fussed over her for a while longer before she shooed them away with a wave of her hands and told them she needed to rest. With the reassurance that their sister was well and settled, John and Michael bid her goodnight and closed her door.

From down the hall she could hear John speaking to Michael. "I hope Wendy's all right."

There was a pause, and then, "I wonder who Peter ended up pranking today. Remember his threat to do some epic April Fool's thing to one of us?" he said dramatically. "Glad it wasn't me!"

Wendy lay breathing slowly, trying to push out the memories from the hill. She realized that her silent prayer had been answered, and she'd been able to defend herself. She'd escaped the dark figure; someone was watching over her. Even on April Fool's Day.

PETER SMILED MISCHIEVOUSLY to himself as he picked up his dark hoodie and climbed into his car to head home. *That's not how I anticipated things would go,* he thought as he rubbed his bruised back gingerly. *But it went better than I planned.* It was clear that Wendy thought of him as her hero once again.

---

## 12

The week flew by, and suddenly it was Friday again. Wendy debated with herself about whether to go to fencing. She'd nearly healed completely from the ordeal on April Fool's. The only evidence that it had happened was a slight limp in her steps (and the horrible memories).

But her hesitancy stemmed from being afraid – and excited – to see Evan again. *Why am I excited to see Evan? Peter proved he's still a hero. Can there be 2 heroes?*

She'd pondered on Evan's story since she'd last seen him. He had stowed away on Peter's ship and left Neverland behind, sought a new life in the real world, reformed from who he used to be, and found work and purpose. Wendy had felt a twinge of jealousy when he mentioned dating, but she'd been the one to ask. She didn't know why she'd asked about his dating life.

*Yes, you do,* her inner voice argued. *You like him.*

*No, I don't,* she argued with herself defensively.

Her inner voice argued back. *Tall, dark, and handsome;*

*those deep blue eyes; his muscular build; and he's not a villain anymore. At least, we don't think he's a villain anymore...*

*You make a good point. Or, I make a good point. Okay, let's just stop this.*

*Then go to class and see him again. Or are you afraid you'll fall for him?*

*Absolutely not. I am not afraid. At all. Of falling for Evan.*

*Prove it.*

*Okay self, I will. And I'll show us I'm not interested in Evan.*

*Sure you will.*

Wendy could almost picture her inner voice smirking at her. She would have a talk with herself later, but for now she needed to get changed for fencing if she wanted to get there on time.

She arrived just before class began. Finding Dave where she'd first met him over by the window, she slipped over and sat down next to him. But bending her knees to sit was still a little painful.

"Hey girl," he greeted. He must have noticed the limp in her steps and her slow descent to sit. "Dude, what happened to you?" he tried whispering, but it only drew the attention of the class and Evan. Evan's face showed concern when he saw Wendy gingerly sit down next to Dave.

"I'll tell you later," Wendy whispered back to Dave.

"That's right, you will," Dave answered with a pointed look.

They were paired as sparring partners, to Wendy's relief and disappointment. She'd felt exhilarated fighting Evan with the fencing foil during the first class, but she knew it was better for her to be partnered with Dave. She interspersed her story of the hill while they practiced their parrying moves.

"Girl," Dave said when Wendy had finished talking. "I'm giving you my number and you had *better* call me if you need someone to escort you to safety again!" He gave her a stern look.

Wendy stood at attention and gave him a salute. "Yes, sir!" she teased.

"I'm serious!" Dave spread his arms in emphasis. "No dude's gonna mess with me. Remember, I've taken Martial Arts." He waved his foil around while doing mock-Karate moves with his arms and making strange noises.

Wendy laughed at his antics. "Thank you, Dave. I appreciate that," she said.

She glanced over at Evan, who was helping a pair of the Spice Girls with the parrying techniques they were learning that day. (Dave had explained to Wendy his reference to the Spice Girls; he'd laughed when she thought it had to do with their fiery attitudes. "No," he said after he'd stopped laughing. "Spice Girls are a band, and one of them dresses all sport-trendy, like these girls do." Wendy made a mental note to look up the band another time.)

Wendy watched as Evan's hand rested atop one of the girl's hands, showing her how to parry. Wendy felt a twinge of jealously. It grew as the girl winked conspiratorially at her partner. Did that girl even need Evan's help? It didn't appear so. Wendy was momentarily distracted by what she saw and Dave won their training match.

"Ha!" he shouted as he punched his fist in the air triumphantly. "Finally got you!" He pumped his fist in the air a few more times in victory, walking in a circle. When he got back around to Wendy his victorious expression faded. "Hey, what's wrong? You always win; don't be a sore loser." He prodded her with his foil. "You even beat me in spite of that limp you got."

"What? Oh! Congratulations on winning." She gave him a forced smile, then looked back at what Evan was doing. Dave followed her gaze and understanding dawned on his face. "Hmmm..." he mused. "You got a thing for the teacher?" he asked, nodding toward Evan.

Wendy whipped her attention back to Dave. "*No...!*" she defended. "Oh bother, I sound just like John," she thought out loud.

"Who's John?" Dave asked. "You got a thing for more than one guy? Make up your mind, girl!" he flung one hand in the air.

This brought Wendy back to her senses, and she laughed at Dave's comment. "No – John is my *brother*, and he says '*no...!*' like that all the time."

"Oh," Dave said in understanding. "But you still got a thing for Evan, right?" he prodded.

"Will you please talk a little more quietly?" Wendy said, pumping her hands up and down to indicate lowered volume. "I really don't want to give anyone that impression. How about we keep practicing?" She tried shifting his attention elsewhere.

"Mmmm...fine," Dave agreed. "But I wanna hear

about this later. Hey! How about I walk you home after?" he offered.

"That would be fine, thank you. Now, let's keep practicing before he notices we've stopped for so long," Wendy pleaded.

It didn't matter. Wendy glanced at Evan; he had seen them talking. And he was headed over toward them.

"Oh, we got the teacher mad," Dave teased, chuckling like a grade-schooler.

EVAN HAD NOTICED Dave and Wendy talking. He wasn't upset about it; the students were adults and could talk if they wanted to. He felt a little jealous at the easy manner with which Wendy and Dave interacted and wished/hoped he could reach that level of familiarity with her. He also wanted to ask about the limp in her step.

As he approached, he heard Dave's comment about "making the teacher mad." Evan smiled at the comment and at Dave's volume. The man truly couldn't whisper.

"How are things over here?" he asked the pair. Wendy scowled mildly at him. Dave just grinned in amusement while looking back and forth between Evan and Wendy.

"Oh, we're *good*," Dave answered, obviously trying to school his expression. "I just beat Wendy for the first time today. Broke her winning streak," he gloated. His face brightened. "Hey! Maybe she needs some help.

Could you show her how to parry properly?" He waved his pointer finger back and forth between Wendy and Evan.

Wendy shot her gaze at Dave, staring daggers at him. He lifted his hands innocently.

"I'd be honored to assist Wendy," Evan agreed. He turned to her and instructed, "Show me your stance."

Wendy looked from Evan to Dave and back again before she did as instructed. Her form looked perfect. *In more ways than one*, he thought. He gave his head a small shake before having her show him how she parried. She looked fine in that, too. *Again, in more ways than one*. He scrunched his face in frustration at his wandering thoughts. *Get it together, Roberts!*

Wendy misinterpreted his expression. "Is it that bad?" she asked, looking worried. "I've bested Dave every time today. I was just a little distracted this last time."

"A *little* distracted?" Dave countered with a raised eyebrow. Wendy scowled at him again and flicked him with her foil.

"Hey! No flicking!" Dave exclaimed. "Just let the man show you how to parry and stop making up excuses. I'm gonna go take a water break." He pointed over to the drinking fountain. And with that, Dave left Evan and Wendy to stare momentarily at each other.

"Here," Evan offered. "This is how you hold the foil when parrying." He stood behind her and put his hand on hers, bringing the foil into position. "Then turn it like this to ward off the attack." Wendy executed the move without trouble, but Evan didn't want to leave his position. The floral scent coming from her skin kept him in place, and the electricity his skin felt holding her hand made him forget how to move.

After a moment Wendy turned her head toward him. Her face was inches from his, and he saw her hold her breath for a few heartbeats while she glanced at his lips. He felt dizzy with the desire to kiss her.

She looked back over to the foil and said to the ground, "I know how to do this, so you can let go now."

Her words stung, though he knew it was the proper thing to do. He didn't want to make her uncomfortable or give the wrong impression to the rest of the class. And he certainly shouldn't kiss her in front of everyone. He took a step back and surveyed the room. The girl he'd been helping earlier stood across the room, arms folded, shooting Wendy a nasty look. *What's that about?*

Wendy must have noticed. She turned away from the girl and faced Evan. He remembered he wanted to ask about her limp. "What happened? It looks like it hurts a little to walk."

She looked down to the ground, then to the other side of the room, as if to avoid answering his question.

"I'm glad you came back to class today," he said in a lowered voice. "I thought...after what I told you last week..." He let the sentence hang.

She looked back up at him, blushing. "You thought I wouldn't believe you," she finished for him. He nodded. Wendy looked into his eyes. "I'm sorry."

A charge passed between them, nearly tangible. He was so attracted to her, and he sensed she was attracted to him, too. He started to say, "Wendy, I..."

Dave came back at that moment, oblivious to the vulnerable mood around them. "Ready to go home? I think the clock says class is over," he said innocently, pointing at the wall clock.

Evan felt a rush of anger at the interruption. In addition to that, he felt a surge of jealousy at Dave's presence. His Hook-temperament surfaced. "Class is over whenever the freak I say it's over," he commanded with a growl. He straightened authoritatively with his shoulders back and scowled at Dave, staring him down.

"Okay...I'll just be over there," Dave pointed to where his backpack lay and skittered toward it.

Evan rounded on Wendy. "What did he mean, 'ready to go home?' Are you allowing *him* to see where you live?" he accused, ticking his head toward Dave and glaring at Wendy.

*I need to calm down. This isn't how I want to be,* he scolded himself.

"As a matter of fact," Wendy said with a haughty air, crossing her arms, "yes. He and I have things to discuss." She lifted her chin and raised that cursed eyebrow at him. Her aim to hurt hit true; his ego and his heart were bruised.

*It's about making peace, not about being right,* he reminded himself. This advice was extremely difficult to follow in the moment, though.

He stared hard at her, wanting to both shout at her and kiss her senseless at the same time. Instead, he shouted, "Class dismissed!" and strode away.

He walked to the back of the room toward the office and hid in there for several minutes, giving the students time to leave before he went back out. He was angry with himself for losing his temper like that. And it had been aimed at Wendy.

*Has she left yet?* he wondered. Giving in to curiosity, he glanced out the office door in time to see Wendy standing at the exit, staring at him. She adjusted the bag strap on her shoulder, then left with Dave.

*Nicely handled, numbskull,* he chided himself. He rubbed the back of his neck with his hand, tilting his head up and squinting his eyes in regret.

## 13

Wendy and Dave headed down the sidewalk toward her apartment. Neither of them spoke for about a block. *Maybe we can walk in companionable silence*, she told herself. Her hope lasted a few more paces before Dave broke the stillness.

"Okay, spill," he said, nudging Wendy with his elbow.

"Spill what?" she asked with feigned innocence. She kept her face forward and started walking a little faster.

Dave whacked her shoulder, tsking at her attempt to dodge the question. "Spill about *you* and *Mr. Roberts* back there!" He pointed in the direction of the Martial Arts studio. "And that look you had on your face when he was helping that Spice Girl in class. You were all like," he mimicked Wendy's facial expression from earlier – scrunching his eyebrows and pouting his lips dramatically.

Wendy laughed and slowed her steps. "I did *not* make that face!" She defended herself between fits of giggles. "It was more like this." She crossed her eyes and stuck her tongue out.

Dave pshaw'd. "You didn't look like *that* either!"

"Oh, we turn left on this street," she instructed while pointing. She took a satisfying breath and let it out. "It feels good to laugh. Thank you."

"You're welcome. But seriously, the face that *I* made – *that's* what you looked like."

Dave followed her lead turning left, heading into a neighborhood. "Nice area," he said as he surveyed the scene. "I love all the trees. But parking's gotta be a nightmare. There's too many cars."

"Parking *is* limited. We try to walk whenever we can. Parking anywhere in this area – including on campus – is rather difficult." Wendy shrugged, resigned to the parking situation.

A few more moments of silence reigned before Dave broke it again. "Okay, no more avoiding the topic here. Do you, or do you not, have a thing for Evan?" He looked down at her with raised eyebrows.

Wendy bit her lower lip, trying to find an answer. "Don't *all* of the girls in class 'have a thing' for him?" she countered with a wave of her hand.

Dave stopped walking; Wendy followed suit. She turned and looked at him, seeing concern on his features. "I know we only became friends last week, but I *am* your friend. You can trust me. I'm not gonna tell anyone or judge you." Dave looked at Wendy with a gentle seriousness that filled her with gratitude. She felt in her soul she could trust him, so she decided to.

She tilted her head to the side. "All right." She began walking again, Dave matching her shorter strides. "Evan and I knew each other from before—"

"I *knew* it!" Dave interrupted, pointing his finger at her. He must have realized his blunder and looked at Wendy sheepishly. "Sorry. I promise I'll be quiet," he said, raising his hand in the Scout salute.

She smiled and continued. "Evan seems to have admirable qualities, and he *is* rather attractive," she smiled wider. "When I knew him before, though, his qualities weren't admirable. They were more...villainous, you could say." She squinted her eyes, testing out the word. "So, while I do find him attractive, and he seems to be a better man, I feel hung up on past memories. Once a villain, always a villain – right?" She looked up at Dave with a questioning look, fidgeting with her hands in apprehension.

"No – no, no, and *no*," Dave said immediately, shaking his head. "People change *all* the time, Wendy. *Every* day. Like my dad. He used to be an alcoholic – he never hurt us when he was drunk, but he did a lot of damage. But one day it's like he woke up to what he was doing, and he said he didn't want to be that way anymore. He got help, he worked hard *every day* to change, and he hasn't had a drop of liquor in *years*! I'm not saying Dad was a villain, but he changed a damaging habit. People can change, Wendy. We make our own choices, you know? And it sounds like Evan is choosing to not be so..." He waved his hand. "villain-ish anymore."

Wendy nodded slowly, looking thoughtfully toward the ground. She wanted to explore that train of thought

– that Evan had changed. She was interested to know where spending more time with him would lead them.

Her musings shifted to Peter. "What about when we choose *not* to change?" she asked, looking up at Dave.

"What do you mean?" he asked with furrowed eyebrows.

She took a moment to put her thoughts into words. "People who have stayed the same for years, though not necessarily in a good way. Does that make them a villain because they aren't improving how they treat others?" She kicked a pebble out of her path.

Dave smirked at her. "You're the psychoanalyst; *you* tell *me*." He bumped her with his shoulder. "But in my opinion," he continued, "I don't think we can divide each other into 'heroes' and 'villains.' We aren't predestined to be just one way or the other." He paused in thought momentarily. "And if we choose not to change things about ourselves that we ought to, then I guess we're missing out on better things."

He looked over at Wendy with a small smile. She could tell he believed what he said, and more importantly, that he lived what he believed.

"This is where we live – my brothers and I." She pointed to the apartment building. "Thank you for taking time to walk me home, and to help me make some sense of things."

"No problem," Dave said. "And I know you already have brothers, but I'm here for you, too." He reached out and gave her an innocent hug. Dave was a true blessing in her life, and she said a silent prayer of gratitude for him.

"Okay girl, I'll see you next week." He started to

turn around, then turned back and pointed at her. "Unless you need an escort to protect you." He did his Martial Arts moves with the strange sounds again.

Wendy laughed and nodded. "I will take you up on that as needed," she said. And with that, she entered her apartment.

## 14

E van watched as Dave hugged Wendy, a spike of jealousy making his scalp tingle. He had debated with himself for about two minutes whether or not to follow Wendy home. Coming to the conclusion that he didn't want to end on the tense note they'd had, he quickly headed out the door and spotted them at the end of the block. He'd kept himself at least half a block away from them, not wanting to be discovered.

He had noticed the playful banter the two shared, as well as when their conversation turned more serious. Envy had begun to fill him, but he kept it at bay with some deep breathing and the thought that Wendy wasn't his, and that giving in to Hook-like anger wouldn't encourage her to want to be around him. He regretted giving in to that anger back at the Martial Arts studio, barking at the class like he used to bark at his pirate crew.

*Making a mistake doesn't undo all I've done to get to this point. Just keep going forward.*

Which is what he did mentally and literally – he followed Wendy and Dave to the apartment. When Dave turned to leave, Evan realized he would likely be seen. Looking left and right for someplace to hide, he ducked behind the back of an apartment building. He peeked his head around after a few minutes to see how far away Dave was; he'd just rounded the corner at the end of the block. Evan let out the breath he'd been holding and felt his shoulders slump with relief. Then he stared at the ground, conversing inwardly with himself.

*Well, now what? Are you good just knowing where she lives or are you going to apologize?* his inner voice asked.

*What if she gets mad at me for following her; it's a bit creepy, don't you think? Also, she already told me in no uncertain terms that she didn't want me to know where she lives,* Evan thought back.

*What if she thinks it's charming that you came all this way to apologize?*

*I could lie and tell her I guessed where she lives.*

*Under NO circumstances will you lie to her. Lies never go well. No lying. Also, that's a terrible lie. There's no way you could guess she lived at THIS exact apartment in a city with THOUSANDS of apartments.*

*You're quite the tyrant. And I know tyrants; I used to be one.*

*I'm not that bad and you know it. Now get over there and talk to her.*

Sometimes Evan really didn't like talking with himself, but most often he found he was the most convenient person to talk to. Hopefully he could change that someday.

He walked around the building he'd been hiding behind and stood next to the street, staring at her door for several seconds. He willed his body to move forward.

*Now or never,* his inner voice urged.

*I choose now,* Evan said back.

He shook his arms out, kinked his neck side to side, and started walking across the street.

"Whoa!" he shouted as he nearly got hit by a passing car.

*Next time, Roberts, look both ways before crossing,* his inner voice chastened.

~

Not long after arriving home, Wendy heard a knock at the door. Thinking it might be Dave, she crossed the room and opened it.

But there stood Evan in her doorway, looking lost and anxious. She felt a thrill at the sight of him, then remembered she had told him she didn't want him to know where she lived. She felt her face heat up and she gripped the door, ready to slam it in his face. He put his hand out and blocked her move, which made Wendy angrier.

"What are you doing here? How do you know where I live?" She hurled questions at him. "Did you *follow* me home?" There was no other explanation; he had to have followed her.

"I..." Evan hesitated, rubbing the back of his neck.

He seemed to be debating with himself. He stared at the ground, then looked up at Wendy, seeming more lost than she'd ever seen him.

She didn't want him to know where she lived. At least, she didn't *think* she wanted him to know where she lived.

"*Well!?*" she prompted vehemently with her hands on her hips.

"I did. I followed you and Dave here," he admitted while still rubbing the back of his neck. "I – I wanted to apologize for losing my temper back there. At class." He dropped his hand and shook his head. "I couldn't leave that between us for another week."

*Did he just say "us"?*

"I'm sorry, Wendy. Both for my temper, and for following you home." He looked genuinely contrite; she'd never seen this look on his face, ever. Captain Hook wasn't contrite; he didn't apologize. But apparently, Evan did.

Wendy stood next to the open door with her arms folded across her chest, feeling a mix of scrutiny and curiosity. Her fear told her to send him away, and her heart told her to let him in. She was just about to make a decision when John and Michael entered the front room from the back of the apartment.

"Wendy, we heard voices. Is everything all right?" Both brothers stood frozen in shock at the sight of Evan. It was the first time they'd seen him since Wendy told them about him a week ago. Once the shock wore off, John scowled and Michael tensed. They walked to Wendy and took a defensive stance, one brother on either side of her. "What do *you* want?" John said rudely, a hand on one hip.

"John – that was impolite," Wendy whispered, turning to him. She wished her brothers weren't home at the moment. "He came to apologize – to *me*." She hoped the implied hint to leave the room didn't escape John's notice. She glared at him, flicking her eyes to the hallway while tilting her head in that direction. John just stood there, oblivious to her hint.

Michael, however, was more perceptive to Wendy's wishes. "John," he said quietly. When John didn't respond (he stood staring Evan down), Michael reached out and tugged him on the arm.

He looked over at Michael. "What?" he asked.

Michael tilted his head to the hallway. John looked confused and shook his head a little. Michael rolled his eyes, then looked at Wendy. "We're going out for a walk," he announced.

"We are?" John said with confusion on his face. He looked from Michael to Evan and back again, as though to give Michael a hint that he wanted to stay.

"Yes John, we're going for a walk," Michael repeated slowly. "Just you and I. Without Wendy. A *nice long walk*." Michael tilted his chin down and raised his eyebrows. And John still stood there, completely missing the point.

"Honestly, John!" Wendy said with mild exasperation, tilting her head back. "He's implying that you leave Evan and me alone to talk."

John looked shocked. "I'm not leaving you alone with *him*!" he argued, pointing to Evan. "Do you forget who he is?"

Evan had watched the exchange between the siblings with amusement until that last comment, which stung. He and Wendy looked at each other. Then glancing between John and Michael, he said resolutely, "That's not who I am anymore." He lifted his hand in surrender. "I left that behind in Neverland. I promise."

"The promise of a pirate – Ha!" John accused, smacking his thigh. "You don't really believe him, do you?" He looked at Wendy.

"I believe him, John; I trust him," she reassured. "At least, I think I do." She bit her lip and looked at Evan. He nodded once, easing Wendy's apprehension.

Michael took hold of John's arm and tugged him out of the apartment, skirting around Evan on their way out. They headed down the block, apparently arguing, if their voices and body language were any indication.

Evan watched them for a few moments. "They care about you; it's apparent in how defensive they are."

"A little *too* defensive sometimes," Wendy said, rolling her eyes. "But they're good men," she smiled. Honestly, she was just relieved they had left. Thank heaven for Michael's intuitive nature.

Wendy looked at Evan who was still standing outside. "So, you *did* follow me here," she said shyly. Now that they were truly alone, and she wasn't angry, she wasn't sure how to act.

He nodded firmly in response to her statement. Her heart began to pound; she felt she could trust him. Which meant that his motives for following her were honest. And that was what she so fiercely wanted – to

know that she could trust him. Because that knowledge
opened up a world of exhilarating possibilities.

## 15

"Do you want to come in?" Wendy asked Evan. She indicated inside the apartment and opened the door wider.

"Yes, thank you," he said, feeling relieved. He entered and walked to a couch in the front room. Wendy sat on the other couch. "What happened with the limp?" he asked while indicating her legs, brows furrowed. "You never got the chance to explain at class."

Wendy gave him an account of the incident on April Fool's Day. He listened with rapt attention, certain his concern was reflected on his face, while his elbows rested on his knees. The further she got into her narrative the more tense and protective Evan felt.

He inhaled deeply to calm down after Wendy finished speaking. He wished he had been there to keep her safe; he wished he could have been her hero.

"Do you know who it was?" he asked. If he ever met

the creep that did that to her – well, he'd probably give the man more than a push, as Wendy had.

"No," Wendy said, rubbing her hands up and down her arms.

Evan sensed the subject made Wendy uneasy, so he focused on her wellbeing instead of the story.

"How are you now?" he asked. He scooted forward on the couch, anxious to hear her answer.

"I'm well enough now," she said, shrugging one shoulder. "Though I've been taking a different route to and from campus – even in the daylight. I guess I still feel nervous about the hill." She looked up at him.

"As anyone would," Evan responded with a cocked eyebrow. "I've heard alarming stories about that hill at night."

"I was in so much pain," Wendy said, squinting her eyes. "I couldn't walk anymore when I reached the bottom of the hill. I'm so glad Peter was there to help me home afterward."

"Peter?" Evan bristled at the mention of his former foe.

*I'm working past that, remember?* he chided himself.

*Peter's a little punk; always has been and always will be,* his inner voice argued.

If Evan could stare down his inner voice he would have. As it was, he did his best to do so internally.

*Fine,* his inner voice concurred. *People can change. But we don't have to like the little –*

"That's fortunate he was there to help you," Evan finally said with a forced smile. "Was he able to get you home safely?" So, *Peter* had been the hero. Evan felt annoyed and envious.

*But it shouldn't matter who got her home, only that she got home without any more harm.*

"Yes. Maybe he's not so bad as I'd begun to think," Wendy said, slightly tilting her head to the side and shrugging a shoulder.

"What do you mean?" Evan asked while leaning forward. Curiosity over Wendy's statement began to push out his annoyance with Peter.

"You know he's always been a bit of a...rascal," Wendy said.

*That's putting it mildly!*

Wendy flopped one hand onto the couch. "I had hoped that when we came to the real world, Peter would finally grow up," she continued.

"Has he grown physically?" Evan asked with interest. "Or is that impossible with his living in Neverland for so long?"

Wendy giggled. "Oh, he's *grown*," she said emphatically with raised eyebrows.

*A bit too emphatically.*

Evan felt his jealousy swell; Wendy seemed to imply that Peter had grown attractively into manhood. He inwardly tamped down the envy and focused his attention on Wendy again.

"So, he can grow *physically*," he reiterated, trying to move forward. "What about *behaviorally*?"

"In behavior..." Here Wendy answered hesitantly. Her eyebrows furrowed for a moment, then she was scowling. Looking back up at Evan, she relaxed her expression and answered, "In behavior, he seems much the same as he was in Neverland."

She looked away. "I'd begun to lose hope that he

would grow up in the maturity-sense – that he would stop acting selfishly and irresponsibly." She shook her head at the words. "But when he helped me home that night – just the fact that he was there. It's begun to change my perspective." She looked back at Evan.

*I can't fault her for seeing good in others*, he thought. *She sees good in me; she should see good in Peter, too.*

"Then we can both have hope that Peter will finally grow up," Evan agreed, trying to push past his jealousy. It would be beneficial for everyone for Peter to grow up. Evan wanted to want good for others. Even if it meant –

"Are you and Peter..." he waved his hand in a circle, not finishing his sentence. He didn't want to outright ask if Wendy and Peter were exclusive. It seemed a bit nosey. He was also extremely afraid of the answer if it was in the affirmative.

"Oh! No," Wendy exclaimed, waving her hands in front of her with an alarmed expression. "Peter and I aren't...He's never...I haven't..." She seemed flustered as she tried to answer the question. She squeezed her eyes shut and shook her head. "I get the impression from him that I'm just 'one of the guys' or a sidekick." She paused for a moment and opened her eyes. She looked at the floor and her face turned murderous as she said, "Though he *certainly* has eyes for *other* girls he sees."

Staring at the floor, she began talking to herself out loud. "Like I'm not even there. Bunch of hussies pass by and he *has* to look at them. No – *ogle* them! Of all the rude and inconsiderate...immature and selfish...Am I that plain looking? I'm not *that* plain," she looked up at Evan, "Am I?"

Her eyes widened. She seemed embarrassed after

she'd spoken her thoughts out loud. She put her head in her hands, like that would make the situation disappear.

Evan was shocked. He couldn't believe she didn't see how stunning she was. He couldn't believe Peter couldn't see that.

*Well, actually I can believe he's blind to that. Blind to anything except himself.*

Wendy was captivating – and strong, intelligent, talented...

*You need to tell her that, Roberts.*

*Right.*

Evan stood and walked to the couch where Wendy sat. She peeked through her fingers and looked at his face. Then she closed her fingers together again, shaking her head. "I'm sorry," she said. "I didn't mean to say all that aloud."

Evan knelt in front of her. "Wendy," he prodded. She shook her head again. "Wendy, do you *really* think you're plain?"

She peeked through her fingers again, looking at him. Evan took one of her hands away from her face. He held it by the wrist gently, setting it on the couch. He scooted closer to maintain contact with her hand and looked her in the eyes. Wendy's eyes widened at his proximity, but Evan didn't care. He wanted to say this to her; he'd wanted to tell her this since before leaving Neverland.

He tilted his chin forward, maintaining eye contact. "You are *astonishing*, Wendy. Your mind, your spirit, the care you give, the work you put into life. It's remarkable." He let go of her hand to pull the other hand from her face. "And as for being plain – a man would have to be blind not to see how breathtaking you are."

"Truly?" she asked incredulously, leaning forward slightly.

"Truly. Peter is more of an idiot than I already knew he was if he can't see your worth. You are extraordinary."

Wendy looked down at the floor, and her blushing face drew Evan closer. When she looked back up their faces were a hand-width apart.

"How long have you felt that way?" she asked quietly.

Evan waited a few heartbeats before answering in a whisper, "A very long time."

Wendy's eyebrows shot up in surprise, but her eyes held Evan's. Her breathing was shallow, as was his.

"Evan..." she began.

"Yes, Wendy." He raised an eyebrow in inquiry.

She inhaled a shaking breath. "Are you going to kiss me now?" she asked, eyes still locked on his.

Goosebumps erupted throughout his scalp. "Would you like me to?" He looked down at her lips.

Her eyes glanced at his lips as well. She opened her mouth as though to answer, then closed it again. "I think so, but I'm not sure." She tucked her lips in shyly, inhaling deeply through her nose.

*That's not the answer we'd hoped for,* his inner voice lamented.

But Evan nodded. "Then I'll wait until you are." He lifted her fingers to his lips, placing a kiss on the back of her hand.

Evan wanted to kiss Wendy *so badly* it was painful

to tell her he would wait until she was ready for him to. Hook would have taken what he wanted regardless of what anyone else felt. But Evan would take things slowly if that's what Wendy wanted.

*Slow and steady wins the race, right?*

*Or wins the kiss.*

"May I call on you again, with permission?" Evan asked after standing.

Wendy smirked up at him. "I believe here it's called 'dating,'" she teased.

"Then I'm asking you out," he said smiling. "Are you free tomorrow?" He held his hand out and helped her stand from the couch.

"I am free, and yes, you may take me out on a date." Her smile widened.

*YES!* both he and his inner voice shouted in his head, and he mentally did a fist-pump in the air.

"Then I'll be back tomorrow." He told her what time he'd come and bowed gallantly before leaving the apartment.

As he stood outside the door, he felt alive and exhilarated. He ran his hand through his hair, his smile stretching the limits of his facial muscles. The results of following Wendy home were worth the risks he'd taken in doing so.

As the euphoria settled down, he looked around and realized he wasn't exactly sure how to get back to the studio. He looked left and right trying to jog his memory, rubbing the back of his neck. He recognized the building across the street that he'd hidden behind. It felt as though it had been hours since hiding there.

Once he got back to the main road just outside the

neighborhood, he was able to figure out the rest of the route back.

On his way home, Evan replayed his time with Wendy over and over in his mind. He was smiling like an idiot when he walked into his apartment, giddy with thoughts of her. The afternoon and evening hadn't gone the way he anticipated; it had gone better.

---

## 16

T he next day dawned dreary and overcast, and by the time Peter got to work that afternoon, it was raining heavily. Heavy rain meant slower business; people weren't as inclined to be playing outdoors when the weather was so miserable.

There were more employees than was necessary for the workload, and 3 of the 6 were sent home. Peter wasn't one of the 3, which meant he got to stay and be around Trina, the tan, dark-haired girl he'd hung out with the previous weekend.

He'd gotten more than he'd anticipated that night. And everything he got was for his gain. He hadn't had that much "fun" for at least a few months. Nothing immoral or scandalous; that wasn't Peter's style. Nor was it Trina's, for which he was grateful.

The third employee was on the sales floor inspecting sports gear and other goods, and being generally available should any customers come in. Peter slipped into the back room where he knew Trina would be working. He looked this way and that from where he stood but didn't see her. Then slender hands turned his shoulders around and pulled him behind the door. Those same slender hands fisted his shirt.

*Ah, there she is*, Peter thought satisfactorily.

Trina stood on her toes and kissed Peter fiercely. He wound his arms around her waist and back, returning the kiss. She nudged the door shut with her foot; it swung closed slowly and quietly. Peter and Trina carried on for several minutes in each other's arms, neither one in a hurry to stop making out in the back room.

*She's good at this. I must be teaching her well. I've always been a good teacher, and I truly like this subject.* Peter inwardly chuckled at his own little joke.

*I wonder what kissing Wendy would be like. I bet she's never been kissed before. Ha! I could be her first.*

Trina finally pulled back from Peter. Her face shone with glee and excitement. "Hi, Peter," she said a bit breathlessly. "I've missed you all week."

"They didn't schedule us together until today," he said disappointedly. "But it makes the time together all the sweeter." He winked at her and kissed her again, but quickly this time.

She giggled girlishly. "You taste like mint," she said while running her hands through his hair.

He flashed her a smile. "I admit, I was chewing gum on my way over," he said. "I had hoped that after work we would pick up where we left off last week, but you started sooner than I anticipated." He gave her a look of mock chastisement. "Rather impatient of you, don't you think?"

She giggled again and pulled him closer. He allowed her some more fun for a few minutes; she really was a good kisser. He wouldn't keep up this charade with her if she wasn't. But the third employee would be wondering where they were soon, and he didn't want to be caught.

He lifted his head away from Trina's and gave her his most charming, roguish smile. He could tell it took her breath away. *It has that effect on all the girls*, he thought cockily.

"We should make an appearance in the front before the other guy comes back here," Peter told her, brows slightly furrowed. "That would be embarrassing for you."

Trina looked surprised. "For me? What do you mean? Why would I be embarrassed to be seen kissing you, Peter?" she asked as she ran her hands over his biceps.

"I'm the one all the other guys hate, remember?" He alluded to the conversation from the previous week. "You'd be tainted by association."

Trina looked at him disbelievingly. "No girl in her right mind would be embarrassed to be seen with *you*, Peter!"

"You're just saying that," he said with feigned modesty, looking at the floor.

"No, seriously!" she countered, swatting his solid chest with her hand.

Their conversation came to a halt when the third employee called to them from the front. She looked at the door and then back to Peter. "I guess we'd better get back out there." She tilted her head to the sales floor.

"I guess we'd better," Peter agreed with another wink.

"Do you wanna...hang out some more after work?" she asked coyly.

"I would love nothing more, my dear." Peter could be charming when he wanted to be. Or when he wanted something from someone.

AFTER OUTDOORS UNLIMITED had been closed and locked up, Peter and Trina went to her place to "hang out." This was where they'd hung out (in the literal sense of the phrase) last weekend when she invited him to spend time with her and her friends.

Peter's thoughts drifted to that night a week ago. He'd felt the vibe that Trina was more than simply being nice by inviting him over; she was attracted to him. He could certainly work with that. He made the first move by kissing her while they went for a walk outside, near her apartment. She had responded in his favor, kissing him back and kissing him a lot.

And all this even though he knew she had a boyfriend.

"My boyfriend would *kill* me if he knew I was with you right now!" Trina had said, giggling and putting her hand over her mouth.

"You have a boyfriend?!" Peter asked, pretending ignorance with wide eyes.

"I thought you knew! I talk about him at work. You need to listen better." Trina played with his ear.

"Oh, sorry. I should go home. I'm so sorry," Peter

said, shaking his head.

"No!" Trina protested. "Don't go. My boyfriend doesn't have to know," she suggested coyly while pulling him closer.

"Well," Peter hesitated. "If you're sure..."

Trina giggled and tugged him in for another kiss.

"Trina?" Peter murmured against her lips.

"Mmm?" she murmured back.

"You're sure he won't find out?" he asked cautiously. He really didn't want to get beat up by her burly boyfriend.

"I'll make sure he doesn't," she promised, pulling Peter closer.

His thoughts returned to the present, though the location and activity were the same as they'd been a week ago.

He thoroughly enjoyed making out with Trina. But he began to grow tired of her company by the end of the evening after work. Since he'd had his fill of her, he decided it was time to move on.

But he was totally unprepared to hear that Trina had broken up with her boyfriend.

"You *what*?!" he exclaimed when she told him.

"Peter," she said, looking shocked by his negative reaction. "I thought you'd be excited." Her face brightened as she went on to say, "Now you and I can be an official thing! The girls at work will be *so* jealous!" She tossed her hair to the side and smiled up at him.

"But what happened with your boyfriend?" Peter's mind was reeling. Now Trina expected to be official with him?! What if her boyfriend came after him?

She rolled her eyes, "He and I had this big argument about something stupid. I figured since he was being all lame about it and you and I have been together anyway...Well, I just broke up with him." She shrugged and looked expectantly at Peter, who felt his irritation written all over his features.

"Peter." She rubbed his arms. "What's wrong? I thought you'd be excited." Her voice was full of disappointment.

"Trina, we're not a 'thing,'" he explained, gesturing between them with his hands and shaking his head.

She laughed uncomfortably, dropping her hands to her side. "What do you mean?"

"This is just NCMO," he said with a shrug, since that was a logical explanation.

Trina looked confused and a bit angry. "What's Nickmo?" she asked with a shake of her head.

Peter laughed at her ignorance. "You've never heard of it? It's totally a thing around here. It's N-C-M-O. It stands for Non-Committal Make Out."

"Non-Committal...Are you *playing* with me?" Trina exclaimed indignantly, putting her hands on her hips. "That's ridiculous!"

"I promise it's a thing. I've been doing it for a while," he waggled his eyebrows. "You have your fun with each other, and then you part ways without any commitment. Move on to the next person."

She looked hurt and confused.

*Not my fault she hasn't heard about NCMO; it's a thing here. She should've known about it. And I can't be expected to stay with one girl for long; where's the fun in that?* he justified to himself.

Trina's face contorted with anger. Her hand flew out

faster than his reflexes could respond, and she slapped him soundly across the face.

"How *dare* you?!" she shouted. "How dare you play with me – with my feelings and my hopes. How dare you play with other girls, and their feelings. You should be so *ashamed*, Peter!" She was huffing and her face had turned red.

Peter rubbed at the place where she'd slapped him. He was suddenly defensive and angry with her. "How dare *I*?! What about you?" He gestured toward her. "You broke up with your boyfriend, not even knowing what *I* would have to say on the matter. If you want to belong to someone so badly go back to him! I can't *believe* you just hit me!" He rubbed the spot again. "And it's not *my* fault you didn't know about NCMO! Go ask your friends – it's real. Don't blame *me* because *you* didn't know!"

Trina took deep breaths, the redness fading from her face. She pointed to the door of her apartment. "Get out," she said evenly. "You are the biggest, most self-centered, immature, inconsiderate, selfish..."

"I get it," Peter interrupted. "You're upset with me." He was tired of hearing her throw rude words at him.

She shook her head. "Just get out, Peter. Go break someone else's heart." She waited until he moved toward the door. The second he was outside she slammed it shut.

*Girls!* he thought. *So touchy and dramatic. I've grown to be quite the heart breaker. Well, I got what I wanted. Ha - the cleverness of me!*

He smiled roguishly and went home, ignoring the niggle of guilt that he refused to give in to.

## 17

Wendy waited in the passenger seat as Evan came around to open her door. *Such a gentleman,* she thought. He'd opened the door for her all evening on their date. Only a few men she'd been on dates with had done that for her. *Must be a dying courtesy; that's a shame.*

Evan opened her door and held his hand out to help her out of the car. They stood there for a moment next to his vehicle – Evan still holding her hand while she looked up at his face. "Are you ready now?" he asked quietly.

"Ready? For...?" Wendy felt a little confused. *Ready to go inside?* she wondered.

He lifted his eyebrows and looked down at her lips. Her neck filled with heat at his implication, and she felt silly for not understanding his question at first. *That's right; he's waiting to kiss me until I'm ready for it.* Her heart sped up at the realization. *Am I ready?*

"Not just yet," she said as she looked down. "And

thank you for being patient." She shuffled her foot around the ground nervously.

She heard him exhale a small huff. "Good things come to those who wait," Evan said. She looked back up at him and smirked. "I'll walk you to your door," he offered, still holding her hand.

They stood below the porch light in front of her apartment. He looked down at her lips again, which sent Wendy into a fit of laughter.

"When I'm ready, you'll know. And I'm extremely impressed at your forbearance, Evan." Wendy bit her lower lip to keep from laughing again.

His expression turned serious. He tilted his chin down and put his hand on her arm. "I spent most of my life selfishly taking what I wanted from others, not giving a care what it would mean for them, or how it would affect them." He looked out to the street, seeming lost in thought. "You have no idea how hard it is to restrain myself and not kiss you breathless, Wendy," he continued, looking back at her.

Wendy's neck once again felt too warm, and tingles erupted across her scalp at Evan's words. She tucked a stray strand of hair behind her ear and looked down at the ground, trying to hide her smile. Evan tilted her chin up with his hand to look at him.

"I am trying *every day* to break old habits and develop better ones," he explained. "I never want to be even a *shadow* of who I used to be. And so I'll keep practicing self-restraint." He smiled and winked at her. "Good night, Wendy," he said as he turned to leave.

"Good night, Evan," she said.

She leaned against the inside of her front door after

closing it. She tilted her head back and sighed content-edly. Her date with Evan had been fun – normal, even!

*I just went on a date with the former Captain Hook!* she thought soberly.

But he was *nothing* like the man she knew in Never-land. The thought gave her goosebumps. She remembered what Dave had said about people's capacity to make a complete turn-around, like he'd said his father had. Gratitude filled her mind as she contemplated how even Evan – the former Captain Hook – had that capacity, and he was doing everything he could to make something of it.

WENDY CHANGED into her pajamas (which consisted of an old t-shirt and some sweatpants) and turned on her Wendy's Mix CD while she waited for John and Michael to come home. As the chorus to her favorite song ("Breathless" by The Corrs) came on, she remembered what Evan had told her about how hard it was to keep himself from kissing *her* breathless. She smiled at the memory and felt her face heat up.

John and Michael came home just then. "Wendy! We're ho-ome!" John sing-songed. "Hey!" his voice turned disapproving. "Are you playing that girly music again?" he called from the front room. Wendy shook her head at his protest. *This is why I only listen to it when they're away*, she thought.

"At least she's not eating popcorn and watching TV again," she heard Michael say, a hint of a smile in his voice.

She came out of her room and greeted them with hugs after turning off the music. "How did your evening go? How was the double date?" She clapped her hands lightly in front of her, excited that her brothers had gone out on dates (something they rarely did).

The brothers looked at each other and smiled. "It went well," Michael said modestly.

"Well?!" John cried, smacking Michael lightly on the arm. "It was *wonderful*!" He punched one fist in the air. "Remember those two girls we told you about a couple weeks ago?"

Wendy nodded. "The one with spunk and the angelic one?"

"Right-O, Wendy!" John confirmed. "They're even more wonderful than we originally thought. So funny, and lovely, and kind, and energetic, and fun to talk to..." his sentence died off as a faraway look took over his face.

Michael and Wendy looked at each other and smiled. "He's quite smitten, it would seem," Wendy commented.

"Indeed," Michael agreed.

"What did you do on your date? Where did you go?" Wendy asked.

John and Michael went into detail about their double date – dinner at a popular local sandwich shop, and a movie at a discount theater nearby. "They didn't even mind that it was a *dollar* theater!" John declared enthusiastically.

Wendy laughed lightly at John's comment; he put so much energy into his words and actions. Then she realized there was a detail she had failed to catch before now. "What are their names?"

"Oh! I guess we should've started with that," John said. "My date's name was Sofia." He turned to Michael and held his hand out in invitation to respond.

"And my date's name was Gina," he said. "They're both from Italy."

"Those are lovely names," Wendy said. "How did you meet them? Are they in any of your classes? Do they live nearby?"

"I wish they lived closer!" John said, waving his hand toward the door. "They live in the foreign student housing area northeast of campus." He crossed his arms and looked put out.

"John, that's hardly far away," Wendy chided, shaking her head.

"Well, it's not like we can *walk* there easily. We had to take the car – and parking anywhere in this neighborhood –"

"Or this city," Michael added.

"–Can be such a pain," John said.

Wendy rolled her eyes playfully. But she fully agreed about the parking bit.

Michael picked up the conversation. "We met them at the campus bookstore; they're both cashiers. John and I were buying school supplies."

Wendy reached out and gave each brother's arm a squeeze. "I'm so happy for both of you. And I'm glad the first date went well," she said. "Do you think you'll ask them out again?"

Michael tried to hide a smile. "Maybe," he said.

"Absolutely!" John answered, hitting Michael lightly

on the arm again. "And a double date again; it's more fun with the four of us."

Michael nodded in agreement and rubbed his arm where John had smacked it. He looked at Wendy. "What did you do tonight?" he asked her. "You haven't been home all evening, have you? We heard you leave earlier, before we left."

Wendy bit her lower lip, smiling as she thought about her date with Evan. Her face began to warm as she swayed her shoulders side-to-side.

"You went on a date," John said with a smile. "You always do that shoulder thing when you like a guy. Who was the lucky duck tonight?" he asked.

Wendy took a breath and held her hands behind her back, still swaying her shoulders. "Evan," she answered, smiling wider.

"The *pirate*?!" John exclaimed. "I thought we'd gone over this already," he said, running a hand through his hair and walking in a circle.

"John," Michael reprimanded quietly with a scowl. He smacked John on the arm, only not lightly.

"What?! I'm her brother; I care about who she hangs out with and who she dates!" John defended himself.

"So do I," Michael said. He looked at Wendy, then back at his brother. "I think you're hurting her feelings, John."

Wendy crossed her arms, her shoulders no longer swaying happily. She stared at John, irritated by his reaction. *Why won't he let that go?* she wondered heatedly.

"He. Is Not. A *Pirate*." She stated each word emphatically. "He is *not* 'Captain Hook.' He is *not* a pirate. He is *not* a villain. He is a *completely* different person, John." She swept her hand out for emphasis. "I hope you'll accept that someday."

John's eyes narrowed in skepticism.

Wendy took a calming breath and uncrossed her arms, placing one hand on John's shoulder. "He can be trusted. He's changed."

"Well," John said, looking around the room as though trying to grasp at anything to justify his position. "What about...Peter?"

"Peter?" Wendy and Michael asked in unison.

"Yes, Peter." John crossed his arms and looked expectantly at Wendy.

"What about him?" Wendy asked in confusion.

"Well, isn't he your hero – your love interest?" John defended.

Michael snorted a laugh but said nothing else.

"Peter?" Wendy answered with a shrug. "Well, he's *Peter*."

"Isn't he anything to you?" John tried.

*For goodness' sake*, Wendy thought. *John is so desperate to take Evan out of the picture that he's proposing Peter as a suitable substitute.* She rolled her eyes.

John hmphed. "Eye rolling is very unladylike, Wendy," he stated. "It doesn't suit you," he said with a sniff.

Belligerence wasn't normally part of Wendy's character, but John's ridiculous stance on the topic of Evan was making it tempting for her to try it out.

So, she did. She took a step toward John and rolled her eyes deliberately in his face.

John gasped. Michael snort laughed again.

"Hook is a bad influence on you, Wendy," John said.

"If only Evan were still 'Hook,' then that would be true," she answered.

"Why not Peter?" John said, a whine in his voice.

"Honestly, John," Michael said, intervening in the conversation. "Wendy has been on his heels for years, and where has it gotten her? He's too much into himself to see her."

He looked briefly at Wendy as if to assess her reaction to his opinion. She nodded, so he continued. "Also, how would you actually feel if he started dating her? Do you see him giving her the attention and credit she deserves?" He lifted his eyebrows in a challenging way, as if daring his brother to disagree with his stance on the subject.

John huffed through his nose a few times, then dropped his defensive position and let a long breath out. "You're right," he said, conceding to Michael. "He's not the sort of man we want for Wendy."

"Or the sort of man that *Wendy* wants for Wendy," Wendy said.

He looked at his sister. "Are you truly over any hopes of 'something more' with Peter?" John asked.

"Mostly," she answered. "I suppose there's still a bit of hero-worship there, but then again, he *is* the hero," she said with a shrug and a smile.

John opened his arms and pulled Wendy in for a hug. Michael joined in.

"I'm sorry, Wendy," John said. He took a deep breath. "I'll try to see something good in Hook—"

"Evan," she and Michael said.

"—Yes, *Evan*," John said. Wendy could hear him rolling his eyes in the way he said Evan's name.

*Reluctantly given or not, it's still a victory*, she thought.

"If that's settled—" Michael said.

"More or less," John put in.

"—Then let's hear about Wendy's date with *Evan*," he looked at John with raised eyebrows.

Both brothers looked at Wendy, who was once again smiling and swaying her shoulders.

## 18

The next week at work Evan was on Cloud Nine every time he thought about his date with Wendy. Or even just every time he thought about her. A few times Coby had to snap Evan out of his thoughts to come back down to reality.

"You're distracted, Evan," Coby observed. "But, like, in a good way. You're smiling more than usual."

Evan's smile grew, glancing at Coby from the passenger seat of the moving van.

"You're right, Coby. I'm distracted in a good way." He wasn't sure what else to say; his thoughts were just a jumble of Wendy.

"You gonna give me details, or will you make me guess every option under the sun?" Coby probed with a teasing tone.

"No guesswork, my friend. I'll tell you," Evan said. He told Coby about the "friend" he'd reconnected with at his fencing class and that they had been on a date last weekend. He sighed contentedly when he finished, putting his arms behind his head. Deciding that was rather uncomfortable in the cab of a moving van, he repositioned them to fold across his chest.

"She sounds awesome," Coby said. "Where do you know her from?"

"You wouldn't believe me if I told you," Evan answered with a humorless chuckle, shaking his head.

*What would his reaction be if I actually said "I met her in Neverland"?* The thought was ridiculous.

"Well, then, what's her name?" Coby asked, elbowing Evan from the driver's seat.

"Her name is Wendy," Evan said, looking at Coby.

"Hey!" Coby seemed very excited and turned to face Evan. "I know a Wendy!"

"Whoa! Eyes on the road, Coby!" Evan pointed to the street ahead. Coby turned back to the steering wheel, looking sheepish.

"Sorry, man," he apologized, then brightened again. "I didn't know there were so many Wendys out there!"

Evan chuckled. *Must be a more popular name than we both thought.*

"Where do you know *your* friend Wendy from?" Evan asked conversationally.

"She's the girl I wanted to set you up with, the girl with the two brothers, two of the guys I went camping with," Coby explained, shrugging.

"Did you all grow up together?" Evan asked, his curiosity piqued.

"I guess you could say that," Coby said, tilting his head from side to side. "Seems like we were kids forever until we all came out here."

"Where did you all come from?" Evan prodded.

Coby looked over at Evan, smiling. "You wouldn't believe me if I told you." He mimicked Evan's voice and answer from earlier.

Evan tossed his head back and laughed. "Your accent is good, Coby." He looked at the street ahead. "You don't think I'd believe you?"

"No, I don't," Coby shook his head, eyes on the road.

"Try me," Evan challenged with a smile.

Coby briefly looked over at Evan, then looked ahead again.

He took in a slow breath and exhaled quickly. "We all came from Neverland," he said with a grimace.

Evan's smile dropped. How would Coby know to joke about Neverland? Maybe a random coincidence?

"I told you you wouldn't believe me," Coby said, looking self-conscious. There was silence in the space between them for several moments before Evan remembered to respond.

"I'd love to believe you," he said. "It's just...it's impossible." He shook his head disbelievingly.

Coby shook his head slowly. "You wouldn't believe what's actually possible, Evan," he said, smiling ruefully. "Ok, I told you where I came from, now it's your turn. After my answer, I'm sure I'd believe anything you say."

Evan debated for a minute on how to respond. *I'm from Neverland. But you weren't there, Coby.*

Or had he been?

Coby glanced at Evan, waiting for an answer. A tense mood had slid in since Coby's response.

*What do I say?* Evan wondered.

*Tell him where you're from; maybe he's not joking. You don't know what happened to all the Lost Boys.*

*The Lost Boys? I think I'd remember them.*

*Would you? Take a better look at him. He said it felt like they'd been kids forever. Sounds like a Lost Boy.*

Evan's debate with himself led him to look more closely at Coby. Strong build, slower mind, curly hair.

*Curly hair?*

*Is that jogging your memory at all?*

*What on earth? It can't be...*

"Curly?" Evan said out loud with disbelief. He squinted his eyes, looking at Coby's facial features. A shadow of the boy Curly was in that face. But how was it possible?

Coby stiffened at hearing the name. He glanced quickly at Evan, a serious look in his eyes. "Why'd you call me that? No one calls me that anymore."

"I think we'd better finish the day's work, then let's talk," Evan said, running his hand through his hair. It was a lot to process. He'd been unknowingly working with one of the Lost Boys for at least a year. But that meant that Coby, or Curly, had been unknowingly working with the former Captain Hook. How would he react when he found out who Evan was?

*Yes, "was.". I'm not that man anymore. I hope he believes me. Dear Lord,* he prayed, *please let him believe me.*

WENDY and her brothers had just finished dinner when there was a knock at the door. John looked up from the sink, where he was doing the dishes. Michael looked up from the fridge, where he was putting away food. That left Wendy, who was still sitting at the table, to answer the door. She stood and walked out of the kitchen.

She was surprised to see Coby on their doorstep. He looked like he'd seen a ghost; his face was pale, his eyes were wide, and he was simply staring straight ahead.

"Coby? Are you alright?" Wendy asked with concern, opening the door wider.

He slowly looked at her, then nodded once. Then he shook his head. Then he shrugged his shoulders.

"Wendy, who's at the door?" John called from the kitchen.

"It's Coby, but he's not looking well," she called back. She held her hand out to Coby to assist him inside. He took her hand, the same shocked look on his face. Wendy walked him over to the couch and helped him sit down. "Do you want some water, Coby?" she asked.

He shook his head, then looked at her. "Did you know...?" he started to ask.

"Know...?" His question was confusing. She needed her brothers for support. "John, Michael, could you come to the front?" she called.

Both stopped what they'd been doing in the kitchen. When they came into the room and saw Coby's expression they hurried the last few steps over to him.

"Coby, mate, what's wrong?" Michael asked, putting a supportive hand on Coby's shoulder.

"He looks like he's going to be sick," John said, alarmed. "Should I grab a bucket or something?" he asked Wendy.

"I don't think that's necessary, John. He asked me something about 'did you know'..." she said.

Coby looked at each of the siblings, one at a time, landing back on Wendy's face. "He's here," he said seriously, his face registering coherence.

"Who's here, Coby?" John asked.

"Hook," Coby answered. "Hook is here. I've been working with him. For, like, a year. Only he's not Hook. He's..."

"He's Evan," Wendy filled in. Her mind was reeling – Coby had been working with Evan? How on Earth?! And neither had recognized the other? How had they finally realized what was going on?

Coby looked up at Wendy, more lucid than when he first arrived. He nodded his head. "Did you know it was him?" he asked.

Wendy nodded. "Yes; John, Michael, and I have known for a few weeks. How is it that you and Evan only *just* put the connection together?" she answered with a question.

Coby shook his head, appearing to clear his thoughts, running his hand over the side of his face. "We got to talking about...Oh!" He pointed to her. "About *you*, Wendy!" he suddenly looked thrilled to have coherent thought back. "We were talking about how he'd reconnected with 'an old friend' and took her out last weekend. We talked about how we both know a Wendy. But it was the same one, you know. And he asked where I came from, so I told him we all came from Neverland—"

"And he believed you?" John interrupted, looking dubious.

"John," Michael mildly admonished, elbowing his brother lightly.

"Sorry," John apologized.

"So, yeah, he believed me," Coby continued. "But he wouldn't talk about all of it until after we finished work. Then it was like—" he made an explosion sound while splaying his hands above his head, his eyes wide.

Wendy fought to keep laughter at bay; Coby's innocence and antics were still as adorable as ever.

"I think," Coby said, "that he didn't recognize me because, you know, I'm all grown up now," he puffed out his chest. "And I don't talk with the accent like the rest of you guys." He sat thinking for a moment, then shrugged his shoulders. "I guess it makes sense."

John shook his head with confusion. "But then, how did *you* not recognize *him*? He looks much the same and sounds much the same. Well, minus the shouting and all that," he finished, waving his hand.

"Um…" Coby seemed to ponder his answer, turning his gaze to the ceiling. "I think it was just one of those out-of-context things, you know?" he said, looking back at the siblings. "I didn't expect to see him here. And he doesn't act *anything* like the Captain Hook we knew from before, and all that." He shrugged.

"Huh," John said, folding his arms comfortably across his chest. "It really is a small world after all!" he said

Coby smiled; Wendy smiled; John smiled at their amusement. But Michael looked troubled.

"Come on, Michael," John prodded Michael's leg with his foot. "All in good fun. Just trying to lighten the mood a little."

Michael looked at Wendy. "Does Peter know he's here? In the real world?" he asked with seriousness.

"No; no, I don't think so. I think if he did, we would know," she responded while gesturing to each of them.

"And he'd kill us if he knew that *we* all knew and didn't tell him," Coby added. "That's gonna be a pain." He shook his head sadly.

"What do you mean, 'going to be'?" John asked.

Coby looked at the siblings. "Well, he's gonna find out, don't you think?" he asked innocently. "I mean, Evan's dating Wendy–"

"They've only been on *one date*," John argued with a scowl, holding out one index finger. Michael thwacked him again for interrupting.

"Sorry, Coby," John apologized.

"He makes a good point," Wendy said, tapping a finger on her mouth. Coby sat up taller and smiled at the compliment. Wendy smiled at him. "I wonder...do we just tell Peter outright? Or wait until he finds out...?" she asked.

*Oh, this just got messier*, she thought to herself.

*You knew that at some point the cat would be out of the bag*, her inner voice answered.

*Yes, well, I haven't wanted to think about it much.*

*What do you want to do?*

*I was hoping you might have some good suggestions.*

*Well, seeing as how we're the same person that might not be very productive.*

*Oh, for goodness' sake! You're no help. Go run some music lyrics through your head, or something!*

Wendy tilted her head back and huffed. It really could be annoying to talk to herself sometimes.

Coby and her brothers stared at her, confusion and curiosity on their faces. She must've been talking in her head longer than she realized.

"Maybe..." Michael began to say.

"Yes, what do you think, Michael," his brother prodded with a nudge.

"Maybe we just let things play out as they will." He shrugged. "If Peter finds out, then all right. If not, maybe we can tell him at some point in the future?" he suggested hesitantly.

Wendy nodded at Michael's idea. Maybe they were making a bigger deal out of it than they needed to.

"Fair enough," John said. "We'll just move forward." He looked around the group. "What's the worst that could happen, right?"

## 19

T he week came and went, with Wendy looking forward to Friday and seeing Evan at fencing again. Each day that passed, she grew more excited. She wondered if he would ask her out again. If he did, she would absolutely say yes. Maybe she would even feel ready for him to kiss her.

Wendy changed into her gym clothes and made a fuss about what to do with her hair and makeup. *Seriously? You're going fencing! You don't need to worry over hair and makeup. Save that for dates.* She nodded at the wisdom of her inner voice and left the bathroom in search of her sneakers. She had just spotted them under her bed when there was a knock at the door.

*Who on earth could that be?* she wondered. *Maybe it's Evan! He's come to escort you to class, or something like that.*

Elated by that idea, she grabbed her shoes and trotted to the door, smiling. Her smile faltered when she opened it and saw Peter standing on her doorstep. She was confused; Peter *never* made spontaneous visits to her apartment.

Peter lifted an eyebrow in irritation, likely due to Wendy's unenthusiastic greeting. "Well, don't look so excited to see me," he chided.

"Oh, I'm sorry, Peter," she said, shaking her head to get the confusion out. "I just wasn't expecting to see you. Please, come in." Wendy opened the door wider and held her hand out to invite him in. He entered, then stood expectantly next to the door.

"You should go get ready," he said, flicking his head in the direction of her room, hands in his pockets.

"Oh. Well, I'm ready," she said, gesturing to her activewear ensemble. "I'm headed to fencing class right now." She pointed toward the front door.

Peter scrunched his face. Then, "Oh! The fencing class! I completely forgot you told me about that." He chuckled. "I guess I'm not going to do that anymore. No hard feelings?" He offered his fist for her to bump.

She fist-bumped him. "No hard feelings, Peter. I figured you'd just forgotten. Don't worry about it."

"I won't," he smiled charmingly at her and took a step forward. "But tonight, you're not going *fencing*. You'll be doing something better." He waggled his eyebrows excitedly at her.

Panic seized Wendy's chest. What was Peter talking about? Had she forgotten some commitment she'd made? What about Evan? She'd been looking forward to seeing him all week.

"What are you talking about, Peter?" she asked, chuckling nervously. She looked around outside since the door was still open. Was he playing some practical joke on her? She needed to leave soon, or she'd be late for class.

Peter pulled his hand out of his pocket with a flourish. In his hand were two tickets. She couldn't see what they were for just yet, as he was waving them tantalizingly from side to side.

"*This* is what I'm talking about. I'm taking you out on a date, Wendy! Ta-da!" He finished with a sweep of his arms out to the side like a showman.

Wendy stared at him in disbelief. "Oh," was all she could manage to say. Peter's thoughtfulness surprised her, arranging things so far as to buy tickets for an event. And there were only two tickets, which meant he wasn't going to take her with a group of other *girls*.

She was also mildly irked that he hadn't asked her beforehand to see if she was available.

"That was very kind of you, Peter," she said. "I'm a bit torn; a date with you is a nice gesture, but I have a prior commitment tonight. It would be better for you to ask me in advance next time."

Peter scowled for a heartbeat then smoothed his features. "Well, I vote that you come with *me* tonight. You can skip one class, you know. It can't be that big of a deal to miss."

*That's the sort of justification that had him failing classes because he skipped out on them all the time!* she thought with increased annoyance.

"Peter," she said placatingly, "I didn't ask for your vote. It was very nice of you to invite me to do something with you, but I'm not available tonight." She looked at him seriously and lifted her eyebrows. "And I need to leave now, or I'll be late for class."

"Wendy!" Peter whined. "Why won't you just come with me?" He sagged his shoulders and huffed childishly.

*He's trying to manipulate me to get what he wants by throwing a fit.*

Wendy stared at him sternly, as a firm parent would with a tantrum-throwing toddler. Peter's face instantly changed from childish-mode to victim-mode.

He straightened from his slumped position. "Wasn't it sweet of me to think of you and get us tickets for the theater tonight?" he said dejectedly. "I had to go all the way to Salt Lake City to purchase these myself." He waved the tickets again.

*Now he's playing the victim. Nice try, Peter.*

Peter stood with an expectant look, watching Wendy for several seconds. Then he broke Wendy's silence and turned defensive. "And I totally already asked you!" He flung his hand toward her. "And you said yes. I think you just forgot." He shook his head as though the fault lay with her forgetful memory.

*And now gaslighting. I certainly did NOT agree to go out with him tonight.*

Peter's manipulative tactics weren't working on Wendy. He must have realized that as he tried a different angle. His face turned contrite as he looked down and dropped his hand with the tickets to his side. When he looked up at Wendy, she wanted to believe the innocence she saw on his face.

"Please, Wendy," he said quietly. "I just want to

spend time with you. I just want to be with you. Please,"
he asked, reaching toward her pleadingly.

His words loosened her defensiveness, a shadow of
her life-long crush on him making its way into her
head again. Maybe it would be good to give him
another chance and spend time with him, one on one.
She would much rather be at fencing with Evan, but
she could tell this would mean a lot to Peter. He was her
friend, after all.

She waited a moment before responding. "All right,
Peter," she said. "I'll go with you." She gave him a polite
smile. "I'll change quickly. Oh! But I need to do something on our way out."

She needed to see Evan; she wanted to explain why
she wouldn't be at class. She didn't want him to think
she'd intentionally ditched him.

Peter's face had brightened dramatically with her
consent to go with him. "We can do whatever you need!
Now hurry, or we'll be late," he said, shooing her with
his hands toward her room.

~

*HA!* Peter thought. *I did it – I bested Wendy! Thought she
could see past my strategies, did she? I'm so clever.*

He rushed her to his car when she was finished
getting ready. For a girl she'd gone quickly. Most girls
he took out spent 2-3 times as much time to make
themselves presentable. Not that they weren't
presentable before; he wouldn't ask them out if they
weren't.

Once she was in the car, Peter sped down her street toward the main road.

"Peter! Slow down!" Wendy said with panic in her voice, clutching the car door with one hand.

"It's fine," he said, waving away her concern. "I know what I'm doing. Now," he decided to change the irksome subject, "are you curious what these tickets are for?" he asked.

"Yes, extremely curious," she responded, exhaling in a huff. "But first, I need to stop somewhere on our way to the theater," she reminded him.

"Oh yes, that's right. Where should I go?" He swept his hand out toward the road.

"To the martial arts studio, where fencing class is," she said, relief in her voice.

He looked over at Wendy with a flash of irritation. "We're back to the fencing thing again?" He rolled his eyes and decided he'd heard enough about that stupid class. "How about I tell you what we're doing tonight on our way there?"

Peter got talking about the grand plans he had for them that evening – dinner at an eclectic new restaurant and then going to Capitol Theater in Salt Lake City to see *The Phantom of the Opera*. He had Wendy's full attention (or rather, he had her distracted) for several minutes. She didn't even realize they were already on the freeway heading north until it was too late to turn around and stop at the martial arts studio.

"Peter!" she cried out in panic, slapping her seat with her hand. "You forgot to stop at the studio! Please, turn around; I need to do something there."

"*I* forgot? I believe it was *you* who forgot to tell me

where it is," he turned the blame on her, lifting his chin with his eyes on the road.

"I can tell you where it is," she said patiently, "but I need you to exit and go back."

He looked at her and said apologetically, "Sorry, Wendy. We have a schedule to maintain if we're to be on time for things tonight." In reality, he wasn't sorry at all for intentionally *not* going where she'd asked him to go. He was so sick of hearing about that ridiculous fencing class.

*What's so special about it, anyway? Nothing that can't take a back seat to an evening with me.*

He could tell Wendy was extremely put out with him and decided to use some of his other strategies to placate her.

"You look lovely tonight; that shade of blue really brightens your eyes. And are those earrings new?" he asked.

She stared at him stone-faced, appearing unamused and unmoved by his flattery.

*Why did she have to study psychology? It's gotten harder to break through her defenses!*

He tried again. "It's a lovely time for a drive; do you see that tree over there? Pink blossoms everywhere on it! The shade of them matches your lips." He turned on his charming smile and looked over at her.

Not only was she still stone-faced, but she'd raised that blasted eyebrow at him. He hated when she did that; it made him feel like he'd done something wrong, and he didn't like that feeling.

*Flattery and distraction aren't making her budge. Why*

*does she have to be so problematic?! Fine; I'll cut to the chase and go straight for contrition. Even though I hate doing it.*

He waited a moment then sighed sadly. He schooled his features to look repentant, dropping his shoulders a little in a show of surrender.

"I'm so sorry, Wendy," he said in a soft voice. "That was important to you, and I got so wrapped up in what I was telling you that I forgot to go to the studio." He shook his head as though berating himself for his mistake. "And now it's too late to turn back; what a mess I've made of things." He scrunched his face, pretending to hold back tears. "Can you forgive me for causing you so much distress?" He looked over at her with a pleading look and puppy dog eyes.

*Come on, Wendy! Take the proffered olive branch and get over your fencing class,* he thought.

Wendy sighed in resignation, her stone-face giving way to a calmer countenance. Her closed-lip smile looked forced, but Peter didn't care.

"Yes, Peter, I forgive you." She took a deep breath and slowly let it out. "It *is* important to me, but how can I fault you for being so excited about this evening's plans? I won't hold that against you. It was an honest mistake." She folded both hands in her lap, turning to face forward.

*That's right, you won't hold it against me!* he thought defensively. *Ha! I've bested her again.*

"Thank you, Wendy." He was done with that conversation; he could only do "contrition" for so long. Being in the wrong wasn't his style.

"So, have you ever seen *Phantom*?" he asked, changing the subject.

"No. But I hear it's amazing!" She lifted her folded hands excitedly. "From what I understand, the story itself takes place around the time I grew up in London. And I've been to the actual Opera House in Paris. Mother and Father took us to the Continent a few years before they died." She sighed contentedly.

"Well," Peter said, "I enjoyed it very much. *I've* seen it before." He turned toward Wendy with raised eyebrows as though she should be impressed with this statement.

"Oh?" Wendy replied, blinking once. "How long ago?"

"About a year ago," he said, smiling and settling into the driver seat more casually, one hand on the steering wheel. "Some friends *insisted* they take me to Vegas to see it; we had a wonderful time," he finished with a chuckle.

"Vegas? How far is it to get there? And which friends did you go with?" she asked, a slight scowl between her eyebrows.

"Wendy, Wendy, *Wendy*," Peter said, waving his free hand. "Vegas is a mere six-hour drive from here. Or faster, depending on who's driving." He looked over and winked at her. Peter didn't like to drive slow, or the speed limit.

"It was with a group of girls from one of my classes last year. I told them I'd never seen *Phantom* and they set about to rectify that." He chuckled again. "Wonderful weekend, that was," he said with a large smile.

When he looked back over at Wendy, her light scowl had turned into a larger one. She folded her arms across her chest and turned toward the passenger side window.

*So touchy! Not my fault no one's ever insisted she go to Vegas for a weekend.*

The silence in the car reigned all the way to the parking lot of the restaurant. Peter put the car in park, turned off the ignition, and sat back in his seat with a sigh. *Why does Wendy have to make the evening difficult? Time for a dose of that charm she shouldn't resist.*

"Wendy, I'm sorry if I said something that upset you," Peter said in a low voice. He reached out and placed a hand on her shoulder. She turned and looked at him. He gave her an alluring, mischievous smile – one that he rarely used on others (though he did use it), and that almost always had Wendy swooning. Her features shifted from angry to deer-in-the-headlights. Then she shook her head and faced out toward her window again.

"You can stop using your tricks on me, Peter," she told him in a soft voice. "I know you use those on other girls to get what you want, but I'm nothing special to you." She shook her head a few times. "You could have any girl you want, and you choose to go through several without any intention of landing on the ground."

She turned to face him, her eyes glossy with tears. "I shouldn't have said yes to you tonight, but I did. So, let's get the evening over with." She huffed out a breath.

Peter was dumbfounded. When had she become so immune to his tactics? *I must've used them on her too many times,* he realized.

Despite her despondent mood, he was still deter-mined to get that #1 Hero spot back. There was one thing he hadn't tried with Wendy, but he'd need to save that amorous tactic for the right moment. For now, he needed to do damage control. He hated damage control; girls could be so high maintenance.

"Get the evening over with? Wendy," he said soothingly, patting her arm. "This will be a night to remember. Just you and me; Wendy and Peter. No other people, no other worries, and no other focus but each other." He raised an eyebrow suggestively. "Let's put the past behind us and go get some dinner. I bet you're hungry; maybe that's why you're having a hard time this evening." He patted her arm once more, unbuckled his seatbelt, and made to open his door.

Wendy rounded on him. "My *hard time this evening*," she said with emphasis, "has *nothing* to do with hunger, and *everything* to do with how insignificant I feel when I'm around you." She waved her hand in his direction.

Peter stopped and turned toward her. "Insignificant?" he asked, genuinely confused. "What do you mean?" *What can she possibly mean?!*

Wendy lifted her chin. "Whenever I'm with you, your eyes can't stay focused on me. They wander to any other girl in your line of sight. And as if that weren't humiliating enough, you go so far as to *flirt* with them from across the room, or even from *right in front* of me." She hit the passenger seat angrily. "And *that* is why I feel insignificant with you, Peter."

She turned her body further toward him and curled her hands around the seat. "Do you realize this is the first time you've *ever* asked me out on a date since we left Neverland?" she asked accusingly.

"But," he said, looking for any way to justify

himself. "We meet up once each month – just you and me! You know, with the fudge and all that," he finished lamely. Those weren't dates, and he knew it.

And he could tell Wendy knew that he knew it, if her dubious expression was any indication.

Time for a tactic change. "Is there someone else?" he accused with narrowed eyes.

"What?" she asked, looking like she'd been blind-sided.

*Good, she's distracted.*

"Are you comparing me with someone else? And I just keep coming up short, don't I?" He shook his head disapprovingly. "Bad form, Wendy. Friends don't do that to each other," he said, folding his arms across his chest.

"What on earth?" she answered, a disbelieving look on her face. "When did this become a problem about...? This has nothing to do with who I'm dating!"

*Hold on! She's dating someone? Like, really dating someone?!*

He felt livid with jealousy. "Did you just say '*who*' you're dating? Who *are* you dating?" he said with a raised voice.

He didn't want to date Wendy, but he had to know who the competition for her attention was. Then he'd do something to set things straight again. He didn't know what he'd do, just that he'd do something. He was quick on his feet; he'd come up with some kind of plan.

"That has *nothing* to do with this, Peter!" she shouted back. "We aren't talking about who I'm dating;

we're talking about how I feel like a nobody when I'm around you!"

Wendy stopped and relaxed her shoulders. She took some deep breaths while closing her eyes.

Peter followed suit. He might not like what he was hearing from Wendy, but he didn't want to shout at her. That made him look like the bad guy.

"But, you *are* dating someone?" he asked more quietly this time, though most of what he said was through gritted teeth.

Wendy scowled. "Is this some sort of love triangle for you, Peter?"

"Just answer the question!" he said, scowling back.

She looked up at him. "Yes," she said unashamedly. "I am."

His scowl deepened. "For how long?"

She looked down at her lap, then out her window. "We've been...reacquainted...for a few weeks."

"'Reacquainted'? What the heck is that supposed to mean? Surely not one of the Lost Boys!" He ran a hand through his hair. "Anyone I know?" he asked, looking out into the parking lot. After a few moments of silence, he turned to look at her.

She looked at his eyes, staring for what felt like longer than it really was. But she didn't answer him directly. "You know a lot of people, Peter." She shrugged, and that was all the answer he got.

"Fine, be that way," he said. "Let's just go get something to eat." And with that, he climbed out of the car.

~

PETER DIDN'T OPEN her door or help her out of the vehicle. Not that Wendy needed help getting out of the car; it was just a polite gesture. Maybe he was too angry to even have thought of it. Wendy sat there a few moments longer after Peter got out. This was ridiculous. She didn't want to fight with him. She could try to be a peacemaker without having him walk all over her. She could at least try.

Dinner went better than the car ride had gone. Bit by bit Wendy tried to be polite. She held her tongue when Peter said something thoughtless. She tried not to bristle each time he flirted with the waitress or other women in the restaurant (and it happened *several* times). Peter was Peter; she should have accepted that a long time ago. It was easier to enjoy the evening when she wasn't giving in to the impulse to be offended.

Soon it was time to head to the theater. Capitol Theater in Salt Lake City was regal and historic. It had been built in 1913 in the Italian Renaissance style and had maintained much of its original charm. Peter had secured them seats in the balcony, where they could see and hear everything clearly. The musical itself was full of emotion and color, with hauntingly beautiful music and a bitter-sweet ending.

Wendy discovered she'd been crying when the curtains fell and the production ended. She searched her bag for some tissues and dabbed her eyes.

Peter looked shocked when he saw her wiping tears away. "It wasn't all that bad!" he said, smacking her on the back.

"Peter, I was crying, not choking," Wendy said, trying to laugh while coughing. "And I wasn't crying because it was bad. I loved it! So much so that it brought me to tears." She stood to leave, but Peter stayed seated.

She glanced down at him. "Did you forget something?" she asked, looking at the floor for anything left behind.

"No," he said, "I just wanted to watch you from down here." He lifted his eyebrow and gave her a cocky smile. He crooked his finger as an invitation for her to sit back down.

Wendy looked at him disapprovingly. She wouldn't be beckoned like that by him. She raised *her* eyebrow in response.

Peter rolled his eyes and stood. "Fine," he said. "Be boring."

She ignored his comment (still trying to make peace), and they walked out to his car.

The ride home was uneventful. And late. Wendy didn't realize how long the musical had been. John and Michael would be asleep by now; she hoped they hadn't been worried about her.

Peter had a hard time finding a place to park along her street, so he drove around the corner and found a narrow spot to pull into. He turned the car off, unbuckled his seatbelt, waggled his eyebrows at Wendy, then got out of the car.

*What was that about?*

This time he opened her door for her and helped her out. When she stood out of the car, he pulled her in tightly and kissed her possessively. Wendy was too shocked at first to stop him. From a distance, she heard shouting and then something crash down the street and her wits caught up with her. She pushed Peter away quickly and forcefully.

"Are you *daft!*" she cried while wiping her mouth with the back of her hand.

"Oh, come on, Wendy," Peter said cockily, dismissing her concern with a wave of his hand. "Admit it – you've wanted me to do that for a *long* time." He gave her a seductive look and reached out to pull her to him again.

She took a step back out of his reach. "Maybe," she said tentatively. Then she shook her head. "But not for the last while. Not anymore." She folded her arms across her chest and took another step back.

Peter scowled. "Since you started *dating* someone?" he shot at her.

She nodded, scowling back at him.

"Fine," he said, standing straighter and fisting his hands on his hips. "You had your opportunity just now. You didn't take it. Fine. Your loss." He dropped his hands and stomped toward the driver's side of his car. "And you're welcome for the fine evening, by the way," he called over his shoulder.

Wendy closed her eyes and shook her head. She hadn't meant to hurt his pride. "Thank you," she said.

He stopped and cupped his hand around his ear. "Sorry, I didn't hear that," he said belligerently.

She huffed. "Thank you for taking me out, Peter. That was thoughtful of you." He had finally taken her out on a date, however self-centered his actions had been.

He turned and walked toward her, his expression smug. "I'll walk you to your door," he said benevolently.

She accepted, and they walked around the corner and down the street to her apartment.

Her brothers had left the porch light on. A note taped to the door read "Wendy." Had John and Michael left her a note? Why not just leave it for her inside? Curious, she pulled it off the door.

"What's that?" Peter asked, nodding to the note.

*That is none of his business!* her inner voice warned.

*It's just a note from my brothers.*

*Don't say I didn't warn you.*

Wendy opened the note; it was from Evan. She quickly closed it back up but wasn't fast enough to put it in her bag. Peter snatched it from her hand and opened it himself.

"Peter!" she chastised. "That's not yours!" She tried to get it back from him, but his reflexes were too quick. He somehow managed to read it even while moving it out of her reach.

When he finished, he looked coldly at her, then thrust his hand forward, returning the note between his fingers. "Who is Evan?" he asked with narrowed eyes.

*Well, crap.*

*I told you!*

Wendy decided to try for nonchalance. "Evan is the man I'm dating," she shrugged her shoulders as though it shouldn't be a big deal.

"As in Evan Roberts, the *fencing* teacher?" Peter asked incredulously.

*He's got a surprisingly good memory,* her inner voice admitted.

*Crap, again! He's going to figure out who Evan is!*

*Not if you don't tell him.*

"Yes, the fencing teacher," she said. She shrugged her shoulders again.

"You said you'd been 'reacquainted' with him; where do you know him from?" Peter interrogated.

Inwardly she huffed. She didn't want to see where this conversation would go.

"Peter, you know a lot of people and I know a lot of people," she gestured between them. She looked at her door and decided it was time for the evening to come to an end. She rushed through her next words. "It's late and I need to go inside. Thank you for a nice evening. Good night."

And though Peter could move much faster than she, Wendy managed to slip inside and lock her door before he could even protest.

*What a disaster*, she thought. She leaned against the door, took out Evan's note, and read it.

Wendy,

I came by to make sure you're alright. I'm still concerned since you weren't at class and you're not home. But if you can make it to the park, the one we walked around that first night, please meet me there tomorrow at ten in the morning.

Yours, Evan

Her heart picked up speed as she read his note. He'd thought of her. He wanted to see her. She felt a thrill thinking of seeing him in the morning and her heart rate sped up further.

*Get some sleep first*, her inner voice encouraged.

Wendy glanced at the clock and winced when she saw how late it was. She felt grateful that Evan had said ten; she could sleep in tomorrow. She got ready for bed, put his note under her pillow, and fell asleep smiling.

PETER FUMED ALL the way back to his car. How could Wendy be like this? How could she have rejected *his* kissing her?! He knew she'd wanted it for so long. And it was the final arsenal he'd been banking on to secure his place on her pedestal again. And it hadn't worked! It baffled him and wounded his pride and ego. He refused to believe he had lost her esteem but couldn't think of what else he could do to become number one in her mind again.

And what had he done to lose that spot in the first place? It must be that blasted Evan Roberts. He'd turned Wendy's head and now Peter couldn't get her to see him as her hero anymore.

Not that he wanted a *relationship* with Wendy. This wasn't some love triangle. He just wanted her highest regard. Even if she had a boyfriend, he still wanted to reign supreme on her list of most important people.

Peter mechanically got into his car and started the engine. He was so lost in thought that he didn't notice the p-thump p-thump sound one of his tires made as he sped down the street. He made it halfway home before the unusual sound finally caught his attention. He pulled over, hopped out of the car with irritation, and noticed his back left tire was completely flat.

*Now this?! What in the world?!*

His tires had been fine all evening. Had he run over

some piece of scrap metal on the way home? Or maybe a nail? He bent down to give it further inspection.

He felt his face heat and his mind filled with fury as his finger traced the long, clean gash in the wheel. Someone had slashed his tire; it was no accident. And since everything had been working properly up until he dropped off Wendy, it had most likely been slashed while he walked her to her door.

## 20

"**W**endy!" John exclaimed. Wendy startled awake and looked up to see her brothers standing over her. She glanced at the clock; it was 6:30 am.

*So much for sleeping in.*

"Where *were* you last night?" John said. "You're usually here when we get home...from anywhere!" he flapped his hands in the air. "Were you alright? What happened?"

"John," Michael prodded quietly. "We'll have more answers if you stop asking her questions." He gave John a pointed look.

"Right. Sorry. Just tell us about last night," John said, looking worried.

Wendy closed her eyes and groaned; she had really been looking forward to sleeping in.

"That bad, huh?" John asked sympathetically.

Wendy shook her head. "No, that's not what I meant. Well, I guess it wasn't a great experience last

night. You see, I was–" Her stomach growled just then.
She needed something to eat before she told them
about her night. "Um, can I tell you over breakfast?" she
asked, putting her hand on her growling stomach.

"Oh! Yes, of course!" John answered right away.
"Michael and I will make something for you. Won't we,
Michael?" He looked to his brother for confirmation.
Michael wore a mix of doubt and amusement on his
face.

"*We* are going to make something?" he asked John.
"Or, *Michael* is going to make something? We all know
you're a disaster in the kitchen, John. No offense
meant." He patted John on the shoulder.

John heaved a sigh. "None taken. I guess I just
offered for *you* to make something, then." He patted
Michael on the arm with one hand and indicated
toward the kitchen with the other. Michael smirked,
and both brothers left Wendy's room for the kitchen.

Wendy took a few minutes to stay in bed, resting for
just a little longer, knowing that she had a few extra
minutes while breakfast was being made. It was sweet
of her brothers – or rather, of Michael – to make something for all of them.

She finally got out of bed, slipped on a pair of socks,
and headed to the kitchen. The apartment filled with
the scent of French toast and scrambled eggs, and her
stomach grumbled just as her mouth began to water.

The siblings sat at the kitchen table and ate in
silence for several minutes. Happy mouths make for
little conversation. Wendy was the first to break the
silence, after drinking some freshly squeezed orange
juice.

Michael, you've outdone yourself. This is fantastic!" She indicated to her plate (which was almost empty by then).

Michael smiled and said a modest, "Thank you" before picking up his cup for his own taste of orange juice.

John, however, was apparently done with talk about breakfast. "Is it Evan?" he asked baldly, placing his palm on the table and looking at Wendy.

Wendy stopped eating, her forkful of eggs halfway to her mouth. She gave him a confused look.

"Glad you like breakfast, too, John," Michael teased.

"Yes, yes, Michael – it's wonderful. It always is." He shot his brother an annoyed look and waved away Michael's comment. Michael just smiled back innocently.

Wendy laughed at the exchange and continued to eat.

"I'm not joking!" John began again, thwapping his hand on the table. "You were out so late; we didn't know when you'd be home!" He spun his hand in front of him as though trying to find more to say. He landed with, "and...et cetera!" He looked at Wendy expectantly. "So, was it Evan?" he waved his hand at her.

Wendy took a breath, collecting her thoughts. She then launched into the events of the past afternoon and evening: Peter insisting she go with him and skip fencing; how he intentionally did *not* stop by class like she'd asked him to; the argument in the restaurant parking lot; having dinner ("What was the food like?!" John wanted to know); the musical at Capitol Theater ("You got to see *Phantom of the Opera*?! Lucky!" John interjected); Peter's kiss when he dropped her off at home—

"He did *what*?!" both brothers exclaimed, John hitting the table again.

"Yes, he did. He kissed me," Wendy said. She put her chin on her hand and rested her elbow on the table.

*Finally*, said her inner voice.

*I know; I've wanted that to happen since I first met him. But...*

*But what?*

*By the time he got around to it, it was not what I wanted anymore.*

*Stupid boy. Sure took his time, didn't he?*

John and Michael stared expectantly at Wendy; she'd become distracted talking to herself.

"What did you do?" John asked, just as Michael said, "Did you like it?"

Wendy grinned at the simultaneous questions.

"To answer Michael's question – I was too shocked to understand if I liked it or not." She scowled slightly. "It was so unexpected that I couldn't think clearly for a moment. And to answer John – I pushed him away once I got my wits back."

Her brothers looked a little confused. "Haven't you wanted him to do that since, well, forever?" John asked, waving his hand in front of him, indicating "forever."

"Yes," Wendy said honestly, shrugging her shoulders. "For years. But he's just been the same since we came here." She shook her head. "No, he's become *worse* since we came here," she amended. "He's grown physically – quite nicely, which is obvious to any girl."

She rolled her eyes. "And he knows that. And he's charming and charismatic. And he's used that to his advantage *several times*." She said the last part through clenched teeth while scowling deeper and curling her fists. "He flirts with anyone he wants, which in and of itself isn't wrong." She placed her hand on her chest. "But it hurts when he does it when *I'm* there with him. Like I don't matter." Her shoulders drooped. "Or more like I only matter when he needs my attention to give his massive ego a boost." She narrowed her eyes and stared at the floor.

When she looked back up, her brothers were sharing a look of worry between each other. Michael put his hand on Wendy's arm. "We didn't know he affected you so deeply in such a negative way," he said gently.

"It's no wonder you didn't want his attention like that," John said. "To have him kiss you after behaving like such a jerk to you. I'd have pushed him away, too." He folded his arms and nodded.

Wendy and Michael both looked at John, smirking. John must have realized the way his statement sounded and waved his hands in the air. "Not like *that!*" he amended. "What I mean is that if a *girl* had treated me the way Peter treated Wendy, then went so far as to kiss me like everything was ok..."

John's harried explanation made Wendy laugh. "We understand you, John." She patted him on the back.

He rolled his eyes at Wendy, who then quoted him from an earlier conversation, imitating his voice. "You shouldn't roll your eyes, John." She wagged her finger at him. "It's ungentlemanly and doesn't suit you, and blah blah blah."

Michael, who had been on the brink of laughter, snort laughed which sent Wendy laughing. John seemed to be suppressing a laugh, so he huffed and crossed his arms across his chest. "You're both incredibly immature," he accused. They continued to laugh.

John huffed again and stood from the table. "Let's get the kitchen cleaned up, shall we? Why are you both still laughing? Don't you have something better to do? Seriously!"

ONCE THE HULLABALLOO in the kitchen had settled down, they all three sat in the front room while Wendy told her brothers about the note Evan had left on the door and how Peter had snatched it from her. She told them what it said – how Evan had missed her at class and wanted to meet with her that morning. She sighed and rested her head on the couch where she sat, smiling at the thought of seeing Evan.

"Quite besotted, isn't she?" John said to Michael.

"Mmm-hmm," Michael said to John.

Wendy pulled her head back up from the couch. She felt herself blushing and smiling hugely.

"Do you think she'll need a chaperone?" Michael teased in mock severity.

"Chaperone?! Michael," Wendy said, sitting up straight. "This isn't the year 1900 anymore." She rolled her eyes.

"Eyes, Wendy," John scolded, but smiled.

Michael snort laughed again.

"No chaperone needed," Wendy said. She looked between her brothers, thinking outside of herself. "What are you boys up to today?" she asked, tilting her head to the side.

John and Michael looked at each other with sappy grins on their faces. Wendy had seen those grins before.

"Hmm," Wendy observed while smirking. "Would your plans happen to have anything to do with two lovely Italian ladies?" She folded her arms comfortably and settled deeper into the couch.

John smiled wider. "Yes, yes they would." He looked at Michael and winked.

"So," Wendy continued, "Gina and Sofia. What plans do you have with them?" Her heart felt light; she was happy for her brothers.

Michael's words were so quiet she almost missed when he said, "I plan to kiss Gina soundly if she'll let me."

"Michael!" John and Wendy exclaimed with shock and amusement.

"I think that's the most scandalous thing I've ever heard you say," Wendy said in mock seriousness, putting her hand to her chest.

John smacked Michael on the back. "All in good time, dear brother. All in good time."

Michael blushed under their attention, but it didn't seem unwelcome.

John turned to Wendy. "In all seriousness," he said, looking quickly at Michael with a teasing grin. "We're spending the day with them, going on a hike and listening to the radio. Or something like that." He waved his hand.

"To be more specific," Michael amended, "we're hiking to the Y on the mountain, then listening to their church's conference via the radio."

"Which church are they affiliated with?" Wendy asked with interest.

"Oh!" John piped in. "The same one we've been going to for those Monday activities – The Church of Jesus Christ of Latter-day Saints. They hold some sort of conference every six months. Gina and Sofia invited us to participate. We're curious what they talk about in these conferences."

Michael nodded in agreement.

Wendy nodded, then turned contemplative. "Also, what does that giant Y on the mountain stand for?" she asked, pointing in the direction of the east mountains. "I think someone explained it to me once, but I've forgotten."

John answered, "It's for the 'Young' in Brigham *Young* University. The hike itself is a series of switch-back trails that span about a mile long." He moved his finger back and forth, indicating switch-back trails. "Shouldn't be too hard, right, Michael?" He looked over at his brother. Michael shrugged his shoulders.

"Famous last words, John," Wendy teased, raising her eyebrows.

"Oh, come on!" John said. "Just a mile! And shouldn't you be getting ready for your date with Evan this morning, or something?"

He shooed her away with his hands, and Wendy skipped down the hallway to her room.

## 21

E van sat on a wooden bench while he waited for Wendy at the designated park. The morning was refreshing – the way spring is pictured to be. Tiny green leaves waking up on trees and bushes; tuffets of grass pushing through the ground; daffodils aplenty, with tulips popping up here and there; dandelions showcasing their bright yellow, unashamed of being weeds; robins hopping around the ground looking for worms, or flying from tree to tree, their chirping a welcome reprieve from the dreadful cawing of the winter crows; and sunshine – so much sunshine.

He crossed one ankle over his other knee, folded his arms across his flat stomach, and leaned his head back to feel the sun on his face. His hair didn't hang over the bench as it would have a few days ago. He'd had it cut short – in fashion with the current style. He wondered what Wendy would think of it. He hoped she would come.

His eyes were closed to the sunlight while his head was tilted back over the bench. A shadow suddenly blocked the sun from his face. He opened his eyes to see what had caused the obstruction, and his heart began to thump against his ribs. The sight of Wendy above him, illuminated by the sunlight behind her, was celestial. She was absolutely captivating to him.

He smiled up at her and she returned the gesture while looking down at him from her vantage point above. They hadn't been reacquainted for long – a few weeks, maybe. But having known her for longer than that, he admired her strength in mind, body and spirit; seeing the care she'd given to her brothers, the Lost Boys, and even the undeserving Peter; and seeing her grow from a sweet girl into this phenomenal woman.

The realization hit him like a cannonball smashing into a ship – he loved Wendy. How long he'd loved her he couldn't determine, but he knew it now.

He raised an eyebrow in question, and she responded with a single nod. He sat up from the bench, turning toward her, while she bent toward him. Their foreheads met in the middle, hesitantly tapping against each other for just a moment.

Then Evan reached his hand behind Wendy's neck to pull her in the rest of the way. Their lips met gently at first. Then it was Wendy whose lips urged his on, and he responded in kind. Her hands went behind his head, threading her fingers through his hair. She stopped their kiss short with a gasp. "Your hair!" she exclaimed.

He pulled her back to him. "Never mind that," he murmured against her mouth. She willingly obeyed and his lips were on hers once more. His heart was beating erratically in his chest, like a sail snapping in a furious wind. He'd wanted to kiss her since first seeing her in his fencing class. He'd nearly been able to do so in her apartment, and it had been physically painful to ask her permission only to have her tell him she needed him to wait. He'd waited patiently until he had her permission to do so. And to say that the wait was worth it was an understatement.

They pulled away from each other, each breathing deeply, but not gasping for breath. Wendy's hands were clasped behind his head. Their noses touched, and their smiles showed how much each had needed that connection. He whispered her name, and she bit her lower lip though her smile widened.

Evan groaned longingly and pulled her mouth to his again. This kiss held no reservation. His mouth moved from her lips and trailed kisses down her chin to her throat, then he made his way back to her passionate lips again. Wendy exhaled a shaky breath as his hand slid up and down her neck. He could feel her tempestuous pulse pound against his fingers.

"I need," she started to say. She eased her head away, inhaling deeply. "I need air," she said through a shaky laugh.

Evan chuckled at her honesty, his hand caressing her face.

"Won't you join me?" He nodded his head toward the bench he sat on.

"And what would you call what we just did?" she asked him with a flirtatious look.

He tossed his head back and laughed at her saucy response. Releasing each other, Evan patted the spot next to him as Wendy walked from the back of the bench to sit next to him.

"You were missed at class last night," he told her.

"I noticed," Wendy said. "I got your note on my door." She turned so she faced him more fully, draping her arm along the back of the bench. "I was impressed that you came to check on me. You didn't have to, but I'm glad you did all the same."

He reached his hand along the back of the bench, fitting her delicate fingers between his.

"When you didn't show up at class, I wondered if you had changed your mind about..."

Wendy attempted to fill in his blank. "About you?" she asked.

"About us," he finished. He held her gaze for a moment.

Then Wendy quirked her mouth to one side. "If you had any doubts before, I hope I've alleviated your concerns with my greeting today." She lifted that eyebrow. He wanted to kiss her all over again.

So, he did. Tugging her hand to propel her to him, he caught her around the back with his other arm and kissed her soundly.

He chuckled when they separated, and her eyes were still closed. "Just making sure," he teased. She opened her eyes, gave him a look of mock-scolding, then scooted closer to him, his arm around her shoulder.

"Where were you yesterday? Did it have anything to do with Peter?" he asked innocently.

She sat forward and turned to look at him. "How

did you know?" she asked with bewilderment on her face.

He pretended to consider how to answer. "Just intuition, I suppose." He looked over at her, barely concealing his amusement.

Wendy sat back, scooted a couple inches over, and folded her arms. "There's something you're not telling me," she said with a curious smile. "Time to 'spill' as Dave would say."

He laughed at her reference to Dave's vernacular. "Let's just say I stuck around for a while after I left that note on your door..." he left the sentence to interpretation and raised his eyebrows.

It seemed to take her a moment to process his answer, then Wendy shot her gaze at him (though not angrily). "You saw Peter walk me to my apartment!" she concluded.

He nodded. "You've always had a quick mind, Wendy."

She snort laughed, then both her hands covered her mouth and nose. "Oh dear, I sound just like Michael," she said behind her hands. She shook her head at herself, then put her hands back down.

"So, you saw how he took your note from me—"

"Blasted rude of him to do so," Evan interrupted gruffly, eyebrows drawn together.

Wendy nodded. "His curiosity seems to compel him to act before thinking," she said. She sat with a ponderous look for a moment, then her hands flew to her mouth again. "Oh!" she exclaimed. She looked at Evan as her face blushed.

*She's adorable when she blushes,* he thought.

*She did that the first time you captured her after she returned to Neverland,* his inner voice answered.

*I know; it was adorable then, too.*

"What has you turning red, Wendy?" he asked.

She lowered her hands. "You saw Peter *kiss* me by his car," she whispered, embarrassed.

Evan's blissful mood turned dark. "Yes; I shouted and kicked a trash can to the other side of the street when I saw him do that."

Wendy's eyes widened in understanding. "That's what that crashing sound was..."

Evan wasn't finished. "It took every *atom* of self-control I had to not run over to him and..." he kicked the foot of the bench with his foot – hard. "That pig-headed, *selfish* mongrel. He didn't even ask you; he just took you and –" he stopped when he saw Wendy's reproachful look.

He took a deep breath to compose himself and cleared his throat, scowling. "Yes, I saw him kiss you." His smile returned at another thought. "*And* I saw you push him away."

Wendy shrugged. "He *was* pig-headed and selfish. He *didn't* ask, and I didn't want him to kiss me. As much as I thought I had wanted him to at one point." She shrugged again. "I'm amazed you didn't do something rash to him."

Evan remained silent, trying (and apparently failing) to appear innocent. He looked at a tree nearby. Wendy moved her head into his line of sight. "Evan..." she prompted.

He looked back at her, shrugging. "What?" he asked with barely concealed guilt.

"*Did* you do something rash to him?" she asked with interest.

"Well," he said, tilting his head side to side. "Technically not *to* him," he justified. Wendy looked at him skeptically.

"Is that right, *technically*?" she asked with narrowed eyes.

His mouth quirked into a poorly concealed smile. "Let's just say he likely had a *low ride* on his way home."

Wendy's jaw dropped and her eyes grew wide. "Did you slash his tires?!" she asked incredulously.

"Just one," he justified, holding up one finger. "One singular tire; that's all."

Wendy shook her head with closed eyes and blew out a heavy breath. "I suppose it could have been worse," she said with a grimace.

Evan stood from the bench. "Let's put that behind us and move forward." He reached his hand toward her, an invitation to stand with him. She took it and stood. Evan kept hold of her hand and bent lower to kiss Wendy's forehead. He straightened and looked down at her; she smiled gently in response.

They walked around the large park in comfortable silence, hand in hand, for a long time.

WENDY WAS LOST in thought as she and Evan strode the perimeter of the park. If anyone had told her before they left Neverland that Captain Hook could reform from villain to – well, not necessarily a hero. She'd learned that people couldn't be divided into only two

categories: hero and villain. But who Evan had become
– the transitions he had undergone and worked for –
were nothing like the nefarious and vengeful Hook.
Wendy looked at Evan's right arm; he didn't even wear
the hook anymore. It made her wonder –

"Evan," she broke their companionable silence
feeling very curious.

"Hm," he responded, looking at her as they passed a
wide sycamore tree.

"Do you still have the…" she found it hard to say the
word, choosing instead to nod her head toward his
right arm.

Evan's mouth twitched an amused smile at her
unfinished sentence. "The what, my dear Miss
Darling?"

Wendy hooked her index finger and waved it in
front of her as though slashing something. Her movement startled a jogger as he trotted past.

"The hook?" Evan clarified with a chuckle. Wendy
nodded. "You can say 'hook,' Wendy," he responded,
giving her a playful expression. "It won't offend me."

"It's more that I associate it with *the man* called
Hook, and you're anything but him now," she
explained. "But yes, that's my question – do you still
have the hook?"

"No." He shook his head. "I left it in Neverland. I
didn't even want to bring it with me when I left." Evan
raised his right arm, examining the stump where his
hook used to be.

"Why?" Wendy asked, head tilted in question.

Evan glanced briefly at a nearby playground
dappled in shade, seeming to contemplate his answer.

Looking back to Wendy, he said, "Too many memories connected to it." He squinted one eye while answering. "Things I didn't want to be associated with. The object that gave me the name that brought fear to the inhabitants of Neverland. I don't want to inspire fear." He ran his stumped arm across the back of his neck.

Wendy processed his answer before responding. "What is it you want to inspire now?" she asked as they turned a corner at the edge of the park.

Evan took a few breaths and looked ahead. "Change," he said. "The kind that looks at life differently, sees it in a broader perspective. Sees that improvement isn't some sort of punishment." He waved his right arm in front of him. "But a gift that the Universe has given us to live life with joy. A gift to share with others while reaching out and helping them do the same, if they're willing."

Wendy thought over his answer, leaning her head against his shoulder as they walked on. She knew there were things about herself that she wasn't quite satisfied with, things she could work on to become a better person. To become more of a benefit to those around her. The list in her head of all the things she wished to fix about herself became long and daunting.

Her countenance must have reflected her feelings because when Evan glanced over at her and saw her despondence, he stopped their walk and turned her to face him.

"What is it?" he asked, searching her face. "Was it something I said?"

Wendy looked up into his gorgeous blue eyes. For a

moment, she forgot what she'd been sad about as they locked gazes. It gave her the strength to answer.

"I was thinking about things I want to alter about myself," she lamented. "The list started to get depressingly long, and the longer it got the heavier I felt." She looked down at the ground, musing over the list again.

Evan tilted her chin up to look at him. "I understand the feeling," he validated. "My 'list' was as high as the sun and deep as the sea at the same time."

"How did you get through it?" she asked with a small shake of her head.

He laughed without humor. "I'm not through it yet, Wendy," he said. "But I know I've come a long way. I just focus on one thing at a time, one day at a time." He released his touch from her chin. "So, no more hook for me," he finished, resuming a lighter tone.

Wendy looked to the side as she considered that for a moment. She turned back to Evan, absorbing his relaxed mood. "Hmm," she said with a touch of humor. "Off the hook." She gave him a teasing smile and tugged on his hand to resume their walk.

Evan laughed, tossing his head back. Then he swung her into his arms, kissed her breathless, and sent fire racing through Wendy's entire body.

## 22

P eter wasn't angry because he'd had to change his flat tire. He wasn't angry because he'd had to pay a pretty penny to replace it. He wasn't angry because of the inconvenience these things caused. He could handle all those things.

What made him angry was that someone had intentionally slashed *his* tire right under his nose. He wasn't accustomed to being the brunt of a prank or vandalism. He was used to being the one *doing* those things.

It festered in him all weekend. And all the week after. His mind was only half present during classes and at work, his mood brooding and uninviting, atypical of his usual confident, flirtatious, and cocky attitude. Final exams were quickly approaching, and he doubted he'd be able to focus on any of them enough to pass if he didn't do something to free his mind from the situation.

So, at the end of the week, he called in sick to work and escaped into the mountains. Nature calmed him; it called to him. And thankfully the weather was agreeable enough to camp in relative comfort. Though honestly, even if there had been a spring snowstorm he would've still sought an outlet in the wild.

He hiked and hiked and hiked, deep and far into the canyon. He wanted to be alone, away from people. Stupid people. People who rejected and judged, who didn't appreciate the efforts he made to capture their attention and good opinion. People who slashed tires at his expense. Peter truly thought highly of himself, but he feared that *others* wouldn't think highly of him. He craved their approval, and he needed their attention. He wanted to be seen as a hero to all.

He was hurting inside, but he couldn't admit that to himself while he was around others. Hence the escape – away from people and into solitude.

He settled himself in a cozy spot far off the beaten track. With his tent set up and a contained fire burning lively before him, he sat on the leaf-strewn ground and let himself think and feel. He let the emotions surge full force through his mind and body. When they became too much to bear, he breathed in deeply and then screamed into the woods, up and away, his voice carried through the trees and beyond.

He heaved a breath, eyes closed, hands curled around the dirt and flora next to him. He dropped his head to his chest and wished he could fly away from it all as he let his thoughts free from the cave he'd held them in.

*What am I doing here?* he wondered to himself. *Why did I leave Neverland? What's my purpose in this place and time?* He let the questions ebb and flow through his mind, whispers of answers forming here and there.

*I wanted to have a new adventure,* he answered himself. *I didn't want to be left behind – everyone else was leaving. Wendy, John, Michael, the Lost Boys. I didn't want to miss out.*

But everyone else had started to move on from the Neverland mindset after they'd landed. They all grew up, found new interests, new places to live, new things to focus their lives on. They didn't need him as their designated leader anymore. It wasn't how he'd pictured it. It wasn't fair! He wasn't needed anymore. That thought grieved him. The pedestal he'd stood on for so long had eroded, and the descent from the top was agonizing.

A tear escaped his eye, rolled down his face, and landed on the ground. He looked down at the spot, then wiped the residual wetness from his face. He'd never cried in front of anyone; never had and never would. Crying was a sign of weakness to him, and he wouldn't show weakness. But holding so much pain inside felt like too much to handle. It was a dichotomy he wasn't able to figure out at present. So, he allowed himself to cry since he was alone. The effect was cathartic.

As the daylight faded, he climbed into his tent, slipped into his sleeping bag, curled up into himself, and fell asleep.

He dreamed he was back in Neverland, and he was the only person on the island. No Indians; no pirates; no mermaids; no Lost Boys; no allies or foes. It was just him.

And apparently the creatures as well. He heard a faint sound – a steady rhythm – coming closer. He soon recognized it as a tick-tock sound. The only thing in Neverland that tick-tocked was the ginormous crocodile he'd fed Hook's hand to. But there was no Hook, so why was the crocodile bothering to come ashore? The sound got louder but he couldn't see the source anywhere.

Fear mounted quickly from the unseen threat, and he climbed high into a nearby tree. The tick-tocking was nearly deafening by that point, and still Peter could see nothing of the croc. Then the sand below the tree moved, vibrating and shaking as though an isolated earthquake were happening in front of him.

The croc pushed its way out of the sand, headfirst. The beast was just as massive as he remembered. At least 30 feet long; sharp, pointed teeth poking out from its mouth; bright green scaly skin (Neverland beasts colored more brightly than creatures in the real world); wide belly splayed on its sides over the sand; and lazy looking limbs (which actually moved much swifter than they appeared).

The croc flicked its tail and looked straight up at Peter. The ticking suddenly stopped, but Peter's heart was pounding – both in the dream and in reality. The croc narrowed its eyes at him, as though assessing Peter.

Peter couldn't stand the tension and terror anymore, and he called out to the croc. "What do you want?!" he screamed. He felt his face contort in furious fear. "Leave me alone! Hook's not here – go somewhere else!" He looked frantically left and right for some sort of escape; he'd always been able to fly away from the beast. But he was trapped up in the tree with the croc below.

The croc shook its head. "Gah!" Peter screamed in alarm. Could the thing really understand what he'd said? If it did, why wouldn't it leave him be? "Shoo! Get away! No Hook here to eat!" He flung one hand to get the croc away. He temporarily lost his balance but caught hold of the tree. The croc shook its head again.

Peter's fear shifted to irritation at not being obeyed. Why would no one do as he wished they would – in reality or in this dream? He hated not having control.

"Are you mocking me?!" he shouted at it. "Think you can make sport of me? I won't be cowed by you! Stay there all you want – I won't let you get me!"

But the croc shook its head again. There was a miscommunication happening. If it really wanted to eat Peter it would've taken more aggressive action by that point.

Peter gave the croc a cautious look. "Are you even trying to eat me?" he called out in a more civil tone. It shook its head. Peter's level of fear dropped several degrees, but he still didn't know what the thing wanted. "Hook's not here; I'm the only person here. Are you looking for him?" he tried. Still a head shake from the croc. That gave Peter pause. Hook wasn't in Neverland. But then, where had he gone?

Peter chewed on this thought for several moments before addressing the croc again. "Where is Hook? Did you already eat him after I left?"

It shook its head.

Peter muttered a curse and looked down at his feet,

processing the answer. He looked back at the croc and asked with irritation, "Well, then where'd he go?"

This time the croc simply directed its eyes upward and lifted its head. Up at the sky, or the clouds, or something that was simply up. "Up?" Peter asked with confusion, still addressing the croc. It nodded its head, then looked back up again.

Peter followed its gaze and saw his ship – the flying one they'd taken to leave Neverland. He stared at it in disbelief. That ship had crashed into irreparable damage when they'd landed in the real world; what was it doing here?

He saw figures standing on it. Two figures. The first he immediately recognized as Wendy – she was the only one in their group with long blonde hair. She was looking up at a dark-haired figure; it only took a second to recognize the second figure as Hook himself.

"Hook's on my ship!" Peter pointed and called out to the croc in anger. "What's he doing on my ship?!" The croc simply indicated back up at the ship, and Peter looked at it again.

What he saw next nearly made him fall off the tree. Hook was kissing Wendy – and she was kissing him back.

Despair filled his whole body. Losing his friend to his *enemy*? What sort of betrayal was this? Not that Peter wanted Wendy in that way, but how could this have happened? How could they do this to him? He didn't deserve this!

"I don't deserve that!" he shouted at the croc, pointing to the ship. Rather than move its head this time, the croc gave him a doubtful look.

Peter reared back. "Oh, *you* think I deserve this, do you? What did I do, eh?"

The croc rolled its eyes, turned around, and walked away.

"Wait!" Peter called to it. "Answer me! What did I do? I need to know! What's happening?!" The croc ambled its way to the water's edge, slipped into the sea, and disappeared under the water. Peter looked up at where the ship had been, but it was gone. He was alone again.

*What did I do to lose a friend over to an enemy?* he contemplated.

The hoot of an owl woke Peter out of his dream. He was sweating and his head and jaw hurt from grinding his teeth in his sleep. He put his hand to his head and groaned. He reached for his water bottle and took a sip to clear his mind.

What had that dream been about? Had he eaten something random that didn't agree with him? What did it mean? Did it mean anything at all? Not all dreams held significance; he'd once dreamed that all he ate was worms, but it was because his stomach had hurt while he'd slept. Was this the same sort of situation?

And Hook and Wendy – of all the ridiculous notions! He laughed shortly out loud, mocking the idea. His sweet and innocent friend Wendy falling prey to the villainous and vengeful Hook. The enemy. He felt grateful in that moment that they'd left Neverland and Hook behind them.

His thoughts turned to the reality of his situation.

His friends had moved on, and he resented it. Wendy was dating someone, and he resented it.

Peter's conscience had never been something he'd listened to, always forcing it away to keep unpleasant feelings of guilt out of his life. But in his vulnerable state, Peter pulled away the barrier and let his conscience fly.

*Why aren't I happy for them?* his conscience prompted. *If I am their friend, why not want something good for them, instead of focusing only on what I want?*

"I *am* their friend!" Peter answered defensively out loud. "I've done so much for them; and look at how they've repaid me!"

Peter heard scurrying outside his tent. Vocalizing his thoughts must've scared away some nearby woodland creature. "Sorry," he apologized.

His conscience continued. *Do I expect them to repay me? Is that what friendship is – expecting their compliance in return for everything I perceive I do for them?*

"Well, give and take, you know," Peter justified out loud, waving his hand.

*And has everything I've done for them been selfless, honest, and kind?*

Peter had no answer to that. Or rather, he had an answer, but he didn't like to admit it. The answer was no. He'd been selfish, dishonest, manipulative, immature, rude; he began to feel heavy under these thoughts and reflections.

"Is this what I did to drive them away? Is this what I did to deserve that wretched dream?" he asked as he stared at his hands. "I don't like feeling like this!" he shouted to the ceiling of his tent.

*Facing the truth is hard.*

"So, it's true, then?" He pounded the floor of the tent with his fist. "I'm just a no-good jerk that no one wants to be around anymore? Well, that makes me feel just *great!*" he yelled sarcastically.

His head began to pound as tears welled up in his eyes. The pain he felt stemmed from feeling rejected and alone. And even more pain stemmed from the weight of his selfish choices stacking on top of each other in his mind. Why was this hurting so much?

*Because I have a conscience, and it's trying to tell me something.*

"And just what is *my conscience* trying to tell me," Peter huffed. He feared what was coming and braced himself for the answer.

*I need to make changes.*

"Argh!" he yelled, running a hand through his hair. He really hadn't wanted to acknowledge that. "I don't want to make changes!"

*If I don't make changes then everything will stay the same.*

"And would that be all that bad?" he challenged.

Peter contemplated his own question. He hated the way things had become – the rejection he felt from his friends, the shallow relationships he formed so he could get things he wanted from others, the burden of guilt that was crashing on him with the realization of his narcissism.

The answer to that last question was yes – if he didn't make changes, it really would be all that bad. He wasn't happy with his current reality, and he didn't want things to remain as they were.

But what could he do about it? The damage had already been done; he'd messed with people's lives in order to satisfy his own desires. Fresh on his mind was his friendship with Wendy and how he'd treated her like she was nothing much to him.

And Trina. He cringed. Not only had he subjected her to NCMO, but he'd done it while she thought they could become something more. He'd broken her trust and he'd broken her heart.

His chest clenched painfully at the distress he'd caused Wendy, Trina, scores of other girls, his Neverland friends – the list extended in his mind. He had to lay down because the anguish of guilt was so intense. It felt like it would never go away and that this guilt would haunt and torment him forever.

"I'm too far gone," he said dejectedly while dragging a hand down his face. "I've been focused only on myself at the expense of so many people! I've done damage – it can't be fixed. It's a hopeless situation." He scrunched his eyes closed.

*What if it's not hopeless? What if things can be fixed? What are the possibilities then?*

These questions gave him pause and he delved into the prospect. If there was something he could do to fix things, would he do it? How would his life feel if things weren't hopeless? What if there was a way to make a turn-around?

The thought of changing suddenly didn't seem so offensive as it had before. He supposed he *could* change. Maybe.

But trying to fix things? Despair found its way in

again because there was no way to fix things. He couldn't even fathom where to start!

*I can start where I am and go one step at a time. I've already made a huge leap by coming to terms with reality and admitting that something needs to change.*

Peter wondered who he would be without the cocky, self-assured attitude he wore everywhere he went, around everyone he met. He looked up and asked himself, "Am I still myself if I change? Do I lose my identity or something? Does my confidence have to go with everything else?"

*I can keep the good and eliminate the bad. Like weeding a garden, pulling one weed out at a time.*

Peter put his hands under his head and stared at the ceiling of the tent. "Like weeding a garden," he repeated. "So, keep my confidence and all that is grand about me, and get rid of the narcissistic traits. And work on it one thing at a time."

Peter felt peace with these thoughts until he remembered the damage he'd done in people's lives. "What about that, though? What about the distress I've caused others? What do I do about that?"

*One apology at a time, try to make things right. I apologize, then it's up to others to choose whether or not to forgive.*

He sat up again and took a sip from his water bottle. His thoughts were spinning and trying to fall into place. They found their bank in his mind one by one and things became clearer.

He had another question for himself, though. "Does that mean I have to forgive others, too? If I'm hoping they'll forgive me?"

*Yes.*

Peter grunted. It meant he'd need to forgive his friends for rejecting him, forgive Wendy for not holding him in her highest esteem, forgive whoever slashed his tire, and forgive –

"No!" he said, shaking his head vigorously. "Not him. I can't ever forgive him." Peter pulled his knees up and wrapped his arms around them, resolutely dismissing the idea of forgiving this single person. "I can't forgive Hook. He is the enemy, and you don't forgive enemies." He sat there, hands fisted and his jaw clenched.

*Even your enemies.*

"Well," Peter said with a scowl and a swipe of his hand. "We'll get to that later, then. I don't want to think about that now."

Despite his resistance to forgiving his enemy, Peter felt peace return when he thought about reforming his ways and trying to mend things with those he'd hurt. It settled over him, his muscles physically relaxed, and his mind cleared of the misery he'd felt mere minutes before. "I think I can do this," he said.

*I can. And things will get better as I do.*

Peter lay back down, hands again behind his head. The thoughts and ideas of change and reconciliation kept him up for a few hours. At some point during his musings, he fell back asleep. This time with no dreams.

## 23

The final weeks of the month of April at BYU always held a certain tension and energy. The *tension* came from the stress of studying for, and taking, final exams. Students spent their time going over information alone or in study groups. As the weather warmed, campus outdoors was strewn about with individuals or groups, textbooks and class notes open, pants rolled up and sandals on feet to soak in the sunshine while reviewing needed information to pass their tests. But despite the sunshine, the stress of testing remained until finals were over.

The *energy* of late April came from the anticipation of graduation ceremonies that followed finals. Graduating students could be seen in the more picturesque parts of campus wearing their graduation robes and caps, pictures being taken to commemorate the occasion. Hotels and restaurants were busy and full of visiting family and friends to celebrate their graduates, making parking in Provo even more aggravating than it usually was.

The days between the end of graduation and the beginning of Spring term were blissfully quiet on campus and in the surrounding neighborhoods. Such was the case for Wendy and her brothers.

During finals, Wendy had tried to spend any free time she had with Evan, but it was difficult with all the necessary studying.

He had tried to help her study one night at her apartment, but they both soon found that they only distracted one another too much for anything productive to happen. ("Must he be *here* when we're trying to study?!" John had protested. Wendy had retorted, "We could always go to Evan's place – *unchaperoned*..." John had ceased complaining after that.)

When the days of finals had come and gone, Wendy found herself with time on her hands before work would begin for Spring term in Professor Brown's office.

"What do you want to do with these free days of yours?" Evan quietly asked her the day after her last final. They sat on a couch in her apartment, perpendicular to where John and Michael sat while they played video games. (Even though it was 10 am. "It keeps our brains active!" John had justified.)

Wendy turned her eyes from the video game to look at Evan. "Don't you have work? And fencing to teach?" she asked with amused confusion.

He shifted his body, angling it toward Wendy. "Yes," he answered, "but I'm off work today, and I'm not working or teaching all day and night. And you've been hard at the academic grindstone; time for a break.

Hence my question: what do you want to do?" he asked, his head tilted curiously.

"You know what they say," Michael said from the other couch while still going at it with the game controller.

Wendy glanced with amusement at Evan before responding to Michael, "What do *they* say, Michael?"

Michael flashed an impish grin. "Work like a *Captain*; play like a *pirate*," he said while still focused on the video game. He turned and winked at Wendy and Evan, who both broke into fits of laughter.

"That's not funny, Michael!" John protested beside his brother. "Also, must Wendy spend *all* her time with Evan?" John countered, also still playing. "What about us?"

After Michael finished sniggering, he darted a glance at John. "What *about* us, John?" he asked. His character in the game was winning.

John was concentrating hard, and it was a few moments before he answered his brother's question, tongue slightly sticking out of his mouth in concentration. "What about Wendy spending time with us? We're loads of fun to be with," he said.

"John," Michael said dubiously, "we're just playing video games."

"Exactly. Nooo!" John exclaimed when Michael's character finished John's off. He turned to Michael as they set up a new level in the game. "She likes watching us play, don't you, Wendy?" He turned and looked expectantly at his sister.

Wendy gave John a skeptical look, then turned to

Michael (who was rolling his eyes). "Eyes, Michael," Wendy imitated John, smirking.

Michael set his eyes straight again. "I hear there are tandem bikes we can rent," he offered. "And Provo Canyon has a trail for bikes and jogging and such. Might be fun."

That sounded fun to Wendy. She turned to Evan, assessing his reaction to the idea.

He didn't look like it sounded fun to him. "I haven't ridden a bike in a *really* long time..." he said.

"Well, you know what they say about getting back on a bicycle," Wendy said with a quirked smile.

Evan grinned sardonically at her evident teasing and asked, "And what do *they* say about that?"

She shrugged and answered, "It's like getting back on a bicycle; you'll get the hang of it again."

"Booo!" John called from his seat. "That was a lame joke, Wendy." He and Michael were once again at it with their video game.

Evan patted her shoulder and gave her a consoling look. She playfully swatted his hand away, then thought the better of it and caught hold of his hand, winding her fingers around his. John happened to glance over at that moment.

"Hey, no PDA in the apartment!" he censured.

Evan turned to Wendy and lowered his voice as he asked, "What's PDA?"

Michael must have overheard the question. "It means – aw John! That move was unfair. Sorry, it stands for Public Display of Affection. Such as hand-holding."

"In that case," Evan said. He pulled Wendy to him and quickly kissed her on the mouth.

"Hey!" John shouted. Michael snort laughed. Evan and Wendy snickered on the couch.

At that moment there was a knock on the door. "Wendy, would you be so good as to answer it? Michael and I are currently otherwise engaged," John said, eyes focused on the game.

Wendy reluctantly released her hold of Evan's hand and went to the door. She was surprised – but delighted – to see Sofia and Gina on her doorstep. They'd met Wendy formally after the excursion her brothers had taken on their hike to the Y. They greeted Wendy enthusiastically with hugs.

Once Michael heard the ladies' voices at the door, he immediately ended his part in the video game. John was a little slower to realize what was happening. He glanced quizzically at Michael, looked over at Sofia and Gina, and quickly ended the game exclaiming, "Oh! Ladies! Just a moment." John and Michael then greeted their guests properly, inviting them to have a seat on the couch. Evan and Wendy scooted over to make room for Michael and Gina; John and Sofia took the other couch.

After a few moments of polite conversation Michael brought up the idea of tandem bikes again. This was met with enthusiastic responses from their Italian friends. Wendy and her brothers turned to Evan, who sighed in resignation. "It seems I've been outnumbered," he surrendered. "Where exactly does one go to rent a tandem bike?" he asked Michael.

Michael looked cautiously at Wendy. "Outdoors Unlimited," he answered slowly.

Wendy bit her lower lip. Evan leaned in and whispered so only she could hear, "You know what that does to me when you bite your lip like that?" he asked with a wink.

Wendy momentarily forgot her concern about Michael's answer and focused on Evan's eyes while tingles spread over her arms. She felt herself blush and bit her lower lip a little harder. Evan groaned.

Michael cleared his throat and Wendy snapped back to reality. He looked at Wendy meaningfully and asked, "Are you still willing to go? I can go inside and get things set up for us, so you don't run into...someone."

Evan looked between the two siblings with confusion. "Am I missing something?" he asked, gesturing between them. Sofia and Gina looked confused as well.

John huffed. "It's not that big a deal!" he said. "He's going to find out about Evan at *some* point." He gave Michael a meaningful look.

Michael seemed to take the hint. "Or," Michael said, apparently backtracking, "maybe he's not even working today." He shrugged like it didn't matter.

Half the group was still in the dark. Evan asked for clarification. "Who is 'he' and why are we avoiding him?" he said to Wendy.

She looked at Evan and answered softly, "Peter works at Outdoors Unlimited." She felt worried. What would happen if Peter saw Evan and did something reckless? Or maybe, like her brothers suggested, it wouldn't be a problem, or maybe Peter wasn't even working there that day.

Evan just shrugged off the tension in the conversation. "I can handle seeing Peter." Wendy looked at him doubtfully. Evan sat up. "I've done it before; I can do it again."

"Yes," Wendy said doubtfully, "tires, and all that."

Evan smirked. Wendy sighed in surrender and stood up. "Shall we be off?" she asked her brothers.

The drive to Outdoors Unlimited was a short one. Wendy rode with Evan in his vehicle; her brothers rode with Sofia and Gina in theirs. They pulled in next to each other in the sparsely populated parking lot and John rolled down his window.

"Will you go in and check first?" he asked, pointing to the store. Michael swatted his brother's arm at the suggestion.

Wendy actually thought it was a good idea. "Yes, I'll go in and ask if he's here. If he's not, then I'll wave you all in or something."

The interior of the store held few customers. Likely, many people had gone out of town after graduation ended. Wendy looked around for Peter without any sign of him. Just to be sure, she approached two girls – clearly employees, evidenced by their name tags and matching shirts – who stood near the register.

She intended to ask if Peter was working there that day. The girls were deep in conversation, and Wendy almost felt guilty interrupting. She caught some of what they were saying as she approached:

"...So glad your schedule is opposite his. I can't believe he did that!" said the girl with blonde hair and blue eyes. Her arms were folded and her fists were clenched.

"He's such a jerk," said the other, who was tan with brown hair. She was leaning her hip against the register counter. Shaking her head she continued, "But that's not even the worst part."

The blonde's eyes widened in disbelief. "Worse than the NCMO?"

Wendy chose this moment to interrupt before their conversation became deeper. She cleared her throat. "Excuse me," she said assertively.

Both employees turned toward Wendy. "Oh! I'm so sorry – it's so slow in here today, and we didn't see anyone come in," said the tan one with a polite smile. Her name tag read "Trina." "What can we do for you?"

Wendy glanced around again for Peter. Still seeing no sign of him she asked, "Is Peter working today? I know it's an odd question..." She stopped explaining at the look of irritation both girls wore upon hearing Peter's name.

Trina's eyes narrowed at Wendy, and she felt alarmed. What had she said to upset these girls so instantly? Was Trina territorial, or something?

"I'm...sorry?" Wendy said lamely, not really knowing what to say.

Trina seemed to snap out of her irritation with a head shake. The other girl, the blonde, put a hand on Wendy's shoulder reassuringly. "It's not you," she explained sagely.

"Sorry," Trina offered, flipping one hand. "It's just... I'm not on very good terms with *Peter* right now." She spat his name out as if it disgusted her. "But to answer your question – no, he's not working today."

"Thankfully," the blonde contributed.

"Oh," Wendy said. Apparently, Peter had gotten on

these girls' bad sides. "Um, in that case, I'd like to see about renting a few tandem bikes for the afternoon."

"Sure!" Trina trotted behind the counter and began paperwork for the rental. Wendy was in the middle of filling out forms when the rest of her group entered the store. She had completely forgotten to wave them in.

"Oh! I'm so sorry, everyone," she apologized, looking up from the paperwork.

John stood beside her and put his hand on her shoulder. "Not to worry, Wendy. When you didn't pop out the door after a while, we figured it was safe to come in," he said with a smile.

"We just need these forms filled out and then Trina," she said nodding her head toward the girl, "will get us set up with everything. She even knows some good trails we can try!" She smiled enthusiastically at the group.

Evan still seemed reluctant to try the tandem bikes. Feeling a bit cheeky, Wendy turned to Trina. "Evan here is a *pro* on a tandem bike," she teased on his behalf. He swatted her hip with his handless right arm.

Trina must've noticed the missing appendage. Her eyes widened a moment before commenting, "That's gotta be quite the accomplishment with just one hand. Anyway," she said, taking the signed forms from Wendy. "I'll take you back to the bikes and you can pick out which ones you want."

The group followed Trina. John and Michael each had their dates' arms linked through theirs. Evan and Wendy walked hand in hand.

Trina waved at the bikes, indicating they had their choice of heights and colors to choose from. "I'll just be

over here, so let me know when you've decided." She
pointed to where the blonde employee stood and
walked over to her.

Wendy conjectured that the girls' conversation
wasn't over yet, as it seemed to pick up where they'd left
off when she'd interrupted them. Though they were
trying to talk quietly, it was about as effective as Dave
trying to whisper. In other words, they weren't quiet at
all. Wendy could overhear every word.

"So, what's the worst part?" the blonde asked, facing
Trina.

"Oh, you're not gonna believe what he did to this
one friend of his," Trina began, folding her arms and
narrowing her eyes.

*I wonder what Peter did this time,* Wendy thought.

Trina continued. "So, Peter has this friend he says
he's known, like, forever," she said to her blonde friend.
"He was all ticked off because she got a boyfriend and
he wasn't her number one hero anymore, or something
like that. So, he disguised himself in a dark hoodie and
freaked her out on Rape Hill –"

Wendy froze, no longer interested in tandem bikes.
Evan paused beside her. "Wendy, what is it?" he asked
quietly. She turned toward Trina and her friend, not
even trying to hide that she was fully eavesdropping.

"What did he do to her?" the blonde asked with
wide eyes.

"Nothing nasty, or anything like that," Trina clarified with a wave of her hand. "He just did something to
freak her out. The girl was so shaken up, Peter said she
landed on her knees and got hurt when it happened.
But she totally pushed him and launched him away

from her," she continued, looking triumphant. "And he landed on his back, and he got this huge bruise and all."

Her friend rolled her hand in a circle. "Then what?!" she prodded.

"And then he acted like some sort of *hero*," she said, using air quotes, "when it was all over. Carried her home or something. I don't know what he's trying to prove." Trina tsked.

The blonde lightly shook her head and then appeared momentarily deep in thought. "But was he a good kisser?" she asked with a smirk.

Trina's smile stretched across her face. "Oh yeah!" she gushed. "*That* part was fun." She turned angry again instantly. "But he was just using me with all that kissing. I didn't even know NCMO was a thing."

"I should've told you about it. Sorry," the blonde said with chagrin.

"No!" Trina fussed. "It's not your fault; it's his!" She waved her hands, then turned somber. "I kinda wish things had worked out. I'm angry, but to be honest I think I still have a thing for him..."

Wendy and her group were all listening in by that point. From the looks on their faces, Evan, John, and Michael were aware that Wendy's experience on April 1st and Trina's account couldn't be unrelated. Wendy's heart rate accelerated as her indignation rose.

All three men began voicing their thoughts at once:

"I can't believe he did that!" John said angrily.

"That was *him*?!" Michael growled.

"When I see that mongrel, I'm going to—" Evan began.

"Stop," Wendy insisted. She inhaled a calming breath. "Let's just stop." She put her hand up placatingly. "Let's get our bikes and just...go." She walked to Trina, ready to be finished hearing any more of her conversation.

But the blonde had another question for Trina. "That poor girl! What was her name?" she asked, her head tilted curiously.

Trina tapped her index finger on her mouth, apparently trying to remember. "Oh, it was something like Windy, or—"

"Wendy," Wendy filled in. "Her name is Wendy; or rather, *my* name is Wendy." She scrunched her eyes closed and huffed, exhausted that this was still a topic of discussion.

The blonde's mouth dropped open. "I didn't know there were *so* many Wendys here!" She placed a hand on her hip and shook her head. "It really is a small world, huh?"

Everyone stared at her for several seconds. She looked around the group and dropped her hand back down. "What?"

Trina opened her mouth as though to enlighten her friend to the situation, but instead pressed her lips together and closed her eyes in resignation.

"I'll just finish up with this group," she said to the blonde. She pointed to the bikes and guided them back that way again. Once they were there she stood awkwardly. Wendy could tell Trina had put two and two together and realized who she was. Wendy decided to address the proverbial elephant in the room.

"I'm sorry Peter used you," she said clumsily. She

really wasn't sure what to say but felt compelled to say *something.*

"Oh, thanks," Trina responded just as awkwardly. "I'm sorry he pulled that awful prank on you."

Wendy wasn't in the habit of carrying grudges. "It's alright, don't worry about it," she said. She looked at her group and saw that everyone except John looked interested in the exchange between Wendy and Trina. John looked like he was spacing out.

"Are we ready to go, then?" he asked, blinking once and pointing to the bikes.

*Always so tactful and perceptive, isn't he?* Wendy thought.

She turned back to Trina. "Water under the bridge," she smiled encouragingly. "You needn't worry about it."

Trina smiled with relief.

Wendy pointed to the bikes as John had. "Shall we?" Trina nodded and the group helped her separate the selected tandem bikes from among the group of others. They wheeled them out the front door as the group discussed taking one of the nearby trails.

Everyone's backs were turned away from the store as they listened to and watched Trina's instructions. She was just finishing up when Evan, who stood next to Wendy, flinched and froze in place.

"Evan, what..." she started to ask. As she turned to look at Evan, she saw Peter standing behind him. With a sword at Evan's back.

∾

PETER HAD COME to Outdoors Unlimited that day intent on apologizing to Trina. It felt like a safe place to approach her. He came in from the employee entrance at the back and asked the blonde employee where Trina was, as he couldn't see her anywhere in the store.

"Oh, she's with a group out front. Getting them set up with tandem bikes," the blonde pointed outside then suddenly appeared defensive. Narrowing her eyes she asked, "Why? What do *you* want with her?"

*Trina must've told her what happened; normally the girls here aren't so hostile,* he said to himself.

He cleared his throat and reminded himself that he'd come to apologize. "I've come to tell her I'm sorry for what I did," he explained with hands out, palms up.

The blonde's face went from prickly to perplexed. "Oh," was all she said. Then, "Ohhhh."

Peter nodded his head. *She must be blonde for a reason.* "I've come to make things right with her. Or, at least *better* with her," he said. The girl pointed toward the front door. Peter gave a slight bow and moved in that direction.

He could see Trina outside giving a group the ins and outs of tandem biking. He felt it would be best to wait for her inside the store rather than interrupt.

He scanned the group outside and was shocked to see John, then Michael, then (*Oh, who are those lovely, exotic-looking ladies? Sorry, stay focused*). He then saw Wendy, who was often to be seen with her brothers. She was holding hands with a tall man with short, dark hair, broad shoulders, and only one hand.

*Hang on – his right hand is missing.* He moved a few steps to the side to catch a glimpse of the man's face. It would be *impossible* for Hook to be with them! But his dream with the croc had him curious and afraid of the possibility, so he walked a little further to investigate.

Shock struck through his chest when he saw the man's face. He knew that face. He *hated* that face. He felt his own face contort in anger as coherent thought fled entirely. Hook *was* here in the real world! It was impossible, but it was reality, nevertheless. And Peter intended to do something about it.

*Remember about forgiving enemies?* his conscience warned.

"Forgiving enemies be hanged," Peter whispered aloud. "He's not supposed to be here."

He whirled around and ran to the back room of the store where odd equipment was kept. He grabbed two swords, one in each hand, then exited through the back, went around the building to the front, and walked slowly toward Hook. When he was within range, he nudged Hook's back with one of the swords. Hook flinched and froze but didn't turn around.

Wendy turned to address Hook, calling him Evan. *Evan? Why doesn't she say Hook?* Her face registered shock upon the sight of Peter and the sword. Peter narrowed his eyes at her. How could she betray him – truly betray him – and befriend his enemy?

## 24

E van didn't know what was poking his back, but if Wendy's facial expression were any indication, it wasn't good. It also hurt; he could feel it beginning to pierce his skin. Wendy looked between Evan and whatever was behind him, her jaw agape and shock in her eyes.

"*Hook*." Even though it had been years since he'd heard that voice, Evan instantly recognized it. It was Peter, and Peter's voice was furious.

"Peter," Evan responded with a bit of heat.

*So, this is how he finds out. Great.* Evan's inner thoughts weren't optimistic. Old sentiments of loathing swelled. He fought them back with deep breaths and rational thoughts. *Let's just see how this plays out, keeping Wendy safe in the meantime.*

Having heard the exchange of names between the foes, John, Michael, and their friends were now riveted on what was happening.

"Is that a sword?" John asked incredulously, pointing behind Evan.

*A sword? That explains the painful poke.*

John turned to Trina, gestured to Peter, and asked, "Where did he get a *sword*?!"

Trina's mouth hung open. "Oh," she snapped out of her shock at John's question. "We keep some odd equipment in the back storage," she explained.

"Yes," John said, "but a *sword*?!" He flung his hand toward the weapon.

"For things like the Medieval Club and stuff like that," she said like it was no big deal.

"Ohhhh," John said while nodding. "I guess that makes sense."

"Yes, yes, we carry swords here!" Peter said with irritation. "Now it's time to see if this *pirate* still knows how to use one." He nudged Evan's back harder with the sword. Evan turned and simultaneously stepped back in one movement, now further away from Peter's weapon. Wendy tugged on Evan's arm, pulling him away.

"Peter, this is ridiculous!" Wendy said incredulously. She looked angry and guilty at the same time, likely because she hadn't thought Peter would find out about Evan like this, either.

"Me?!" Peter yelled at Wendy. "*I'm* ridiculous?!" He pointed to himself. "You know what's really ridiculous? Having a *friend* turn on you, taking sides with the *enemy*!" He shot his finger out, pointing at Evan. "And *romantically*, even! It's not only ridiculous, Wendy, it's shameful – it's betrayal!" Peter's face was a mix of rage and pain. "YOU NEVER. EVEN. TOLD ME!"

Evan had noticed John and Michael inching their way over to Peter, probably to try to take the weapons from him. But Peter's reflexes had always been quick, and he shifted position to point the other sword at them. They jumped back, hands placating Peter.

"No need for violence, Peter," Michael said calmly as he slowly stepped away.

Peter looked to Evan before responding, "I'll have it all the same. Just like old times, eh, *Captain!*" He flipped the sword at Evan, who caught it deftly with his left hand. Evan moved quickly away from Wendy to keep her out of harm's way.

Evan wasn't keen on fighting Peter – with or without a sword. But if Peter wanted a fight, Evan could hold his own. The tricky part would be fighting without his hook – he'd never fought Peter without it. But Peter had always been able to fly during their battles – something he lacked the ability to do here.

*This should be interesting*, he thought.

They circled one another, swords out, feet moving purposefully. Evan angled his steps away from the group and into the open empty space of the parking lot, and Peter followed.

Evan didn't want to deliver the first strike. That had always been his style during their fights in Neverland. He'd been blinded by anger and hate for Peter, thirsty to cut him anywhere he could with the sword or his hook.

Memories of that hate surfaced, and Evan worked to suppress the feeling. He could see the hostility and loathing in Peter's expression, and from what he could remember of their battles, Peter was stronger when his emotions were so heated.

Peter's steps slowed and then stopped. He bent his legs as though preparing to spring forward at any moment. Evan braced himself, positioning himself likewise. Without warning, Peter shot forward, swinging his sword toward Evan's head. Evan blocked the move, but just barely. Peter shot back again, only this time he sprang forward sooner, taking aim at Evan's left hand. Evan blocked this also.

Peter no longer spent energy to spring forward and shoot back; he came at Evan directly, slashing his sword this way and that. It should have been a foolish move – haphazard and clumsy. But Evan knew that Peter knew what he was doing, since he'd done it several times before. And Evan knew how to parry and block the mayhem.

Peter pressed upon Evan – swing, clash, bang, swing, ching, swing, clash!

Peter swung high; Evan bent backward from the waist to dodge. Peter swung low; Evan tuck-jumped over Peter's weapon. Peter growled in frustration. Evan swung low, and Peter flipped backwards in the air, agilely landing on his feet.

Trina clapped in the distance. "Go Peter!" she shouted. "Wait," she asked the group, "who are we cheering for?" There was a collective groan.

After one especially heavy and heated thrust, swinging his sword down and across at Evan, Peter and Evan battled from a standstill, pushing against each other's swords, weapons locked in place. Evan felt tension from head to toe. He could imagine how he and

Peter must appear – the strain on their faces from the exertion, the flexing of muscles, how their feet gripped the ground to stay rooted to the spot.

"WHY ARE YOU HERE?!" Peter screamed in Evan's face. "You're supposed to be back in *Neverland*! How dare you follow me! And HOW DARE you turn my friends against me!" His words and voice were so intense that spittle flew from his mouth with each syllable. Fury etched every line of Peter's face, and he was panting – likely from the strain of the battle, his anger, and his screaming.

Evan became defensive. "I DIDN'T FOLLOW YOU!" he yelled back. His hackles rose at Peter's accusations – especially at the notion that he had turned Wendy against Peter. Peter had done that all on his own. Evan refused to be leveled with that charge.

Peter took a deep breath. "YES! YOU! DID!" he screamed. The force of his anger was enough to thrust Evan away.

Evan stumbled backward a few steps and fell, throwing his right arm back to brace for the impact. He landed on his elbow, pain shooting up his arm. Peter came at Evan again, swinging another blow down at him. Evan blocked it, but it was more luck than skill considering the position he was in.

"Bad form!" he heard John shout from the group near the store with his hands cupped around his mouth. "NEVER attack a man when he's down! *You* taught us that, Peter!"

Peter sobered a degree and stepped back, still panting from the fight. Evan was able to catch his breath and jump up to standing. He could feel the warm drip of blood coming from his right arm.

As Peter's breathing slowed enough for him to talk, he asked again, only not screaming this time, "Why are you here, Hook? *How* are you here?!" His sword was still up, ready for battle, but his body language showed no sign of imminent attack.

Evan took the opportunity to answer. Scowling, he said, "I stowed away on your ship."

Peter barked a humorless laugh. "*You*?!" he pointed at Evan. "The great *Captain Hook*, stowing away on a ship?! That's *pathetic*, Hook!" Peter swung his sword in a circle at his side, then leveled it at Evan. "Though I suppose that answers the How. Now answer the Why – why are you here?" he asked through gritted teeth.

Evan closed his eyes and took a breath to clear his head. Being called "pathetic" never made anyone feel good. He opened his eyes and exhaled the anger he felt. Peter's eyes were narrowed in suspicion, as though he didn't trust the answer coming.

"I..." Evan began. He gave his head a quick shake. "I wanted a new start. A new life. I was tired of being the 'villain.'"

Peter fumed. "No!" he shouted, lunging forward and attempting to skewer his sword in Evan's abdomen. "You're *lying*!" Evan parried the attack and expertly stepped to the side and out of range of Peter's sword.

"Once a villain," Peter said accusingly, "*always* a villain! There's no new *anything* here for you!" Clash, swing, clang! He pressed upon Evan again, moving them further through the parking lot.

Evan resented Peter's response – his belief that

villains couldn't change. Evan *had* changed; he *had* a new life – a wonderful one. One that involved friends, honest labor, and Wendy.

*Wendy.*

Evan stopped short in their battle. He had a few choice words he wanted to say to Peter about Wendy. Peter had had his turn to air his grievances. With his sword kept protectively in front of him in his left hand, he pointed his right arm toward Wendy. "What about Wendy, Peter?"

This made Peter stop short also. "What about her?" His face scrunched in confusion.

"You've been her hero for ages, Peter—" Evan said.

"And I still am!" Peter interrupted, shouting.

Evan shook his head. "But what sort of *hero* orchestrates his friend to be followed and become terror-stricken as a *prank*, Peter?" he pressed.

Peter scoffed and waved his free hand. "It was just—"

"And treats her as anything less than the *indescribably* amazing woman she is? Flirting with *other girls* in front of her?" He gestured to Wendy again. "Pursuing other relationships when you *knew* she wanted you? How is that heroic, Peter?"

Peter looked between Wendy and Evan, scowling. "But I—"

"And what of the other people you've used to obtain your own means?" Evan continued, sweeping his arm out to encompass others.

"Yeah!" Trina shouted from the group, arms folded and hip jutted out in feminine hostility.

Peter's scowl deepened. "Enough – from all of you!"

he called as he waved his sword around at everyone present. He lowered the sword, the end of it touching the ground.

Evan sensed Peter might be willing to listen, so he forged ahead as he regained his composure.

"Everything I've done since arriving here," he said, his voice even, "*everything* I've worked for has been to leave the villain behind and discover a life without anger and hate. The hook is still in Neverland – physically and symbolically." He lowered his weapon as well. "I've worked in honest labor, I've a good place to live, I've made friends—"

"*My* friends!" Peter interrupted, pointing to the group.

Evan ignored the accusation and kept going. "I am *not* who I was. People can change – for good or worse. *I've* changed, Peter!"

His sword now hung limp in his hand, and he had no intention to raise it unless to protect himself. "I've also learned how to forgive. I've forgiven myself." He leveled his gaze at Peter. "I've forgiven you." He took a cleansing breath. It was healing to say those words aloud to Peter in person.

Peter scoffed again. "*You* forgive *me*? Ha!" He flipped his sword overhead and caught it without looking. "What have you to forgive me for, Hook?" he said with conniving amusement.

"His name is Evan!" Wendy called out.

Peter turned to the group. "Will you lot just stay out of this!" he called in exasperation.

After a few seconds – "No!" John called back.

Peter rolled his eyes and faced Evan once more.

*John always was rather belligerent,* Peter thought with irritation.

Though Peter hated to admit it, what Hook had said was true – Peter had been a poor example of a hero. He'd come to realize that in the woods a few weeks ago. He had come here today to apologize to Trina – he was attempting to right the wrongs he'd done. But he didn't like to hear a recounting of his faults from the likes of Hook. That was insanely aggravating.

Battling had felt good. Peter hadn't fought for such a long time, but he took pride in seeing he "still had it," as the saying went. But at some point during their fight, Peter had sensed a difference in Hook's manner and had lost the desire to continue battling. Fighting *this* version of Hook was nothing like fighting the Neverland Hook.

He didn't want to believe that Hook could change – he wanted someone else to be the villain so he wouldn't feel so bad about his own faults. But he understood that was a selfish way to see the world – that as long as someone else was worse than you, you didn't need to change anything or feel guilty for what you did.

A large lump had lodged itself in his throat. It wasn't the impulse to cry – he didn't cry in front of others. It was fear. He was afraid to confess and own up to his mistakes. He was afraid to believe Hook wasn't a villain anymore. He was afraid of entertaining the notion to forgive this man before him. Wouldn't that make him weak?

But Peter wanted to make things different in his life. He was worn out from self-centeredness.

*Just like Hook was worn out from being a villain*, he realized.

He felt his expression sober. He breathed in deeply, trying to calm his mind. He'd taken risks before – wonderful, thrilling, adventure-strewn risks. But he was terrified of the risk he was about to take. He was terrified of vulnerability.

"I'm..." He lifted his chin in a last-ditch effort to maintain his pride. "I know that what I've done has been...wrong." He ran his hands through his hair in agitation. This was harder than he thought.

"And I'm..." he flung his hands in the air and took a quick breath to get the words out. "I'm sorry!" He shouted it, then his whole body deflated. He dropped the sword and kicked it away.

He looked up at Hook, or Evan, or whatever he called himself now. Evan's face was shocked. Peter looked at the group. Wendy's hands covered her mouth and nose, and it looked like her eyes were tearful.

John's mouth looked like a large "O" and his eyes were wide. Michael and their exotic friends each held sober expressions.

Trina's hands covered her mouth, and her eyebrows lifted. When she saw Peter was looking at her, she dropped her hands from her face, revealing a smile.

*Smiling?* And then she waved at him. *What the heck?*

Peter looked back at Evan since Trina was too confusing to watch at the moment. Evan had tossed his sword on the ground, and he now strode forward to Peter. Peter wasn't sure what to expect, but it certainly wasn't for Evan's hand to be outstretched, inviting a handshake. Peter took a half-step back and eyed Evan warily. Old instinct told him not to trust this man who looked like Hook but behaved like someone different.

*I've already taken a big risk today. Why not one more?* He shrugged, sighed, and clasped hands with Evan.

Somewhere between his apology and the handshake, Peter felt a weight lift from his soul. He couldn't remember ever feeling this light – in Neverland or the real world. It was more liberating than flying.

## 25

Wendy had thoroughly enjoyed their bike ride through Provo Canyon. She and Evan were the first of their group to return to Outdoors Unlimited. John, Michael, Gina, and Sofia had stopped along the trail to take pictures and admire a particularly scenic vista near Bridal Veil Falls – a waterfall about a mile into the canyon. They had told Wendy and Evan to continue on.

As Wendy and Evan approached the building, they slowed their tandem bike and halted in the parking lot. Wendy's heart raced from the exercise, and she took some deep breaths before dismounting. She turned and looked at Evan, who was grinning from ear to ear.

Wendy's mouth quirked to the side, and she raised an eyebrow. "That wasn't so bad, now, was it?" she prodded.

Evan shook his head, then stared at Wendy's mouth. "You know," he said as he took a step toward her. "When you quirk your mouth like that it reminds me of something I need to do." He took another step closer.

Wendy straightened. "Oh," she said curiously. "And what is that?" She tilted her head to the side as she watched him approach.

"I'll show you." Evan closed the distance and pulled her toward him in one movement. Then his lips were on hers – firm, warm, and intense. Wendy let out a sigh and deepened their kiss. Her hands slid up his strong arms and she wound her arms around his neck. He held her securely around her waist, his hand splayed over her lower back. Wendy quivered and he pulled her closer, a deep groan sounding from his throat. Her hand slid into his hair, which was wind swept from their ride.

Everything in this moment felt whole to Wendy. Everything in her world came into alignment. Had they not gone with Peter from London to Neverland after her parents' death, and had they not made the journey back to the real world from Neverland – there was so much she would have never experienced.

Had she not woken to the reality of Peter's less than desirable behavior toward her (which she fully forgave him for), her mind would never have been opened to the possibility of Evan in her life. And had she not risked trusting this man who held her adoringly, her life would be incomplete. She was grateful she'd had the faith to trust; to say it was worth it was a massive understatement.

Wendy and Evan gently broke apart, foreheads resting against each other, inhaling deeply to catch their breath. She looked up and saw him watching her.

He gave a breathy chuckle, which she reciprocated. His hand cupped her face and he kissed her nose. His blue eyes held hers for several seconds, and the look he gave her – how would she describe it? Valued, appreciated, needed, wanted. Loved.

*Loved!*

Wendy held her breath when that realization hit her. A warm thrill shot through her from head to foot. She bit her lower lip to keep from smiling too big. Evan looked down at her lips again, raised his eyebrow, and kissed her gently. All that she had been through was truly worth being where she was in that moment.

EVAN COULDN'T HELP WANTING to kiss Wendy any time she did something with her mouth, like smirking or biting her lip. Really, he just loved kissing her. He loved this woman.

*When do I tell her that I love her?* he wondered.

He didn't want to scare her off. Not that Wendy was fragile or fickle. He just wanted to follow her lead. Unless it took too long; then he'd just have to take the risk. But for today, for now, this was right.

"Hallooooo!" he heard John call from a distance. Evan and Wendy both turned toward the greeting. John and Sofia were swiftly approaching, with John waving his hand in salutation. They rolled to a stop near Evan and Wendy, then dismounted.

"That was thrilling!" John exclaimed while pumping his fist in the air. Sofia echoed the sentiment. She stepped up next to John and held one of his arms with both her hands, an enchanted smile on her face. John looked down at her and his face split in a huge grin. These two made a sweet couple.

Wendy looked behind them, her eyes scanning the distance. "Where are Michael and Gina?" she asked. "We thought they'd be right along behind you."

John and Sofia looked behind them and shrugged at each other. "They kept pace with us for most of the journey," John said. "Then about a mile ago they stopped to look over a bridge and Michael waved us on. They should be along soon. I mean, how long can they stare at a river?" He scoffed and looked as though the thought were ridiculous.

Sofia, however, had her hand over her mouth and stifled a laugh. John looked down at her. "What?" She simply shook her head and giggled.

Wendy looked behind her brother and his friend again, shading her eyes with her hand to look for Michael. Seeing nothing, she lowered her hand. "Shall we take these in, then?" The group nodded in agreement and headed inside.

As Trina had been the one to get them set up, Wendy scanned the store for her. She saw no Trina, but instead found the blonde from earlier. Wendy approached her and asked for Trina.

"Oh, she's not here," the girl said, leaning her elbow against the register counter. Then she just stood there as though that answer was sufficient.

Moments of silence followed.

Evan cleared his throat. "We simply asked for her because we need to return the bikes," he explained.

"Would you be so good as to help us finalize the rental return?"

A light bulb seemed to go on in the girl's head. She jumped to attention. "Oh! Sure. I can do that!" She waved them in the right direction and led the way.

They got everything settled within the store, and just as they were leaving, Michael and Gina rolled into the parking lot.

John tossed his hand in the air. "Where have you been?" he called out. "We've already finished with everything."

Michael stole a glance at Gina, whose face was a blushing shade of pink. Looking at John, he answered, "The view from the bridge was...breathtaking." He looked at Wendy meaningfully. Her eyes widened in understanding. Gina beamed at Sofia, who gave a quiet squeal.

*What was that?* Evan wondered.

*Just ask Wendy later,* he answered himself.

John looked between Michael, Gina, Sofia, and Wendy. "What?" he asked cluelessly with wide eyes.

Michael cleared his throat. "Anyone up for a movie?" he asked, changing the subject. "I hear there's a good one about Caribbean *pirates* that just came out." He looked at Evan and smirked.

Evan took the good-natured jab and laughed. "My curiosity is piqued," he responded with a mischievous grin. "All in favor say 'aye.'" Everyone except John agreed.

"That's not funny, Michael," he whispered loudly. Sofia nudged John, still holding onto his arm, and commented on how she'd love to see a movie with him.

"Well then..." His whole demeanor shifted to suit her opinion. "Let's be off! And," he said with enthusiasm, "let's not forget the movie food!" He rubbed his hands together. "Some licorice sounds excellent after all that biking!"

## 26

P eter had been confused by Trina waving and
smiling at him at the end of "the final battle."
Peter had begun to think of the sword fight
with Hook – no, Evan – as a final battle. He didn't *hate*
Evan anymore. Though he didn't really *like* him, either.
But Evan wasn't Hook; he'd sensed that during their
fight and had come to see more of that afterward.

The group had parted awkwardly from him, riding
off toward the canyon. Trina remained, still smiling at
him. Her smile and the little wave she'd given him had
thrown him off. Hadn't she made it perfectly clear how
angry she was with him? He didn't blame her; he'd
used her horribly.

But there she was, the only person remaining after
Wendy and the rest of the group left. Peter thought it
would be appropriate to approach Trina and apologize
more formally than the "I'm sorry!" he yelled at
everyone earlier.

So, he walked toward her hesitantly, dragging a

sword in each hand. (He wanted to put the swords away. It felt like the right thing to do, seeing as how he'd been the one to bring them out in the first place.)

As he got closer to Trina she started bouncing on her toes, hands clasped in front of her chest, another smile on her face. Peter stopped and looked at her, feeling confused.

*What is she doing?* he wondered.

He looked behind him; maybe she was getting worked up about someone else. When he turned back around, he saw her trotting toward him.

Peter's reflexes were extremely quick, but nothing could've prepared him for the tight embrace Trina gave him when she reached him. He dropped both swords, a loud clang ringing against the building. He stood there with Trina's arms wrapped around his own. He looked down at her and she tilted her head up.

"I forgive you, Peter," she said as a smile widened across her tan face. Relaxing her hold on him, she took a half-step back and looked at him earnestly.

He felt his eyebrows shoot up in shock and his head reared back slightly. "You do?" he said incredulously. "Already?"

Trina nodded her head emphatically, her lips pulled in. She bounced on her toes again.

Peter's relief was immediate. He felt his face break into a grin – a wholesome, unselfish, non-conceited grin. To be forgiven was a spectacular adventure.

Trina looked down, then to the side, then back up at him. Or rather, at Peter's mouth. Then, looking into his eyes, she asked shyly, "Can we start over?" Her feet had stopped bouncing, but one foot timidly scuffed the ground, turning side-to-side from her ankle.

"Trina," he said, "I should be the one asking you for a re-do." He felt at a loss for words. "How should we begin?" he asked sincerely.

Trina's toes began bouncing again. She unwound her arms from around him and gripped the front of his shirt. On a final toe-bounce she closed the distance between their lips. Her kiss was earnest and short.

"How about a walk?" she suggested as she drew away.

Peter huffed a laugh; he had *not* been expecting that. Not after what he'd put her through. He nodded at her suggestion.

"It's almost time for my shift to end anyway," she justified with a shoulder shrug. "I'll just go clock-out." She nodded her head toward the building.

Peter cleared his throat. "And I'll just...go put these away," he said, nudging one sword with his foot.

She released her hold on his shirt and he bent to pick the swords up.

"I didn't know you could use a *sword*," she said in amazement, putting one hand on her hip.

Peter stood holding both weapons. "It's been a while since I've used one," he responded. It felt good to wield one again.

"It was *so hot* watching you out there!" Trina gushed. She then wrapped one hand around his bicep as they entered the building.

Peter puffed his chest out a bit. The pride inside him felt different than before. It was more like a swelling gratitude mixed with a desire to make the girl next to him happy. "I'm glad you enjoyed the show," he said while winking at her.

She stopped short. "That was just a *show*?!" Her mouth dropped open and her eyes widened. "Wow! I didn't know you guys did that professionally! We should get a group together or something and you guys could totally perform."

They resumed their walk, Trina waving her free hand as she continued talking. "Oh! Or you could teach the Medieval Club! They would *so* love that!" She twittered on all the way back while she clocked-out, and all the way back while Peter put the swords away. And for a good while on the walk she'd suggested, her hand in Peter's while they strolled toward nowhere in particular.

Peter supposed that some men might find her chatty and somewhat silly nature to be bothersome. But it suited Trina. Peter found it attractive and endearing. He could see them dating in earnest this time – no more NCMO or flitting about from girl to girl. No more flirting with any and every pretty female around him.

Who knew? Maybe there was a future with Trina. He smiled down at her and she beamed up at him.

"I DIDN'T KNOW you'd cry through the movie," Wendy said to Evan, hitting his arm playfully. "I'm all out of tissues now." She barely contained a snicker, putting her hand over her mouth.

"I was *laughing*!" Evan said defensively. He looked down at Wendy as they made their way through the movie theater halls. "And I wasn't the only one; your brothers took their fair share of tissues."

They both looked behind them to see John and Michael with Sofia and Gina. Her brothers were still wiping tears from their faces and getting the last of their laughter out.

"*See!*" Evan waved his hand toward them. "You did plenty of laughing, too, you know," he said as he tossed an empty box of popcorn into a nearby trash can.

"Nice shot," Wendy praised. Evan shrugged a shoulder with a mildly cocky grin. Wendy finished the last of her soda with a loud slurp, then took aim at the same trash can – and missed by at least two feet.

Evan, gentleman that he was, detoured his steps to pick up the cup and finish the job. Wendy scowled at him for a moment, then softened and thanked him. Evan gave a gallant bow. "You're a genius with a sword, Wendy, but you've got terrible aim." He shook his head in mock sorrow and she reached out to hold his hand.

Wendy sighed. "It's true enough, so I won't deny it," she said while swinging their joined hands.

"Watch this!" they heard from behind them. They stopped their walk and turned. John wadded up his box of licorice (which was more of a crumpled mass than a ball), took aim, and shot the box toward the trash can as one would shoot a basketball. It also landed several feet from the intended target.

John grunted. "I meant to miss, just so you know," he said without shame. He trotted over and threw the box away.

"Right," Michael said quietly from behind John.

"Is poor aim genetic, then?" Evan asked the group.

Michael then took his box of popcorn, upended it to empty the rest of its contents into his mouth, and while still chewing, threw the box straight into the middle of the trash can. Gina and Sofia clapped approvingly. Michael bowed modestly while John said something under his breath about "showoff."

"Does that answer your question?" Michael said to Evan, mouth half-full of popcorn.

Wendy laughed, Evan saluted Michael, and the group resumed their walk toward the exit.

"Well," John said as they left the building, "those were some of the *worst* pirates I've ever seen!" He shook his head matter-of-factly. "So much bumbling around – especially the Sparrow one. But..." He lifted his hand and pointed with his index finger. "It was *extremely* entertaining!" He smacked his thigh for emphasis.

"It was just a movie, John," Wendy pointed out with a giggle. "Also – you, Michael, and Evan all owe me more tissues." She looked at each man in turn.

"And they don't know what pirates were *really* like back then," Wendy continued, nudging Evan and sending his steps to the side. He chuckled lightly.

"Not many people do," Michael said. Gina alluded to how nobody would know *exactly* what a pirate's life would've been like, since no one had been alive that long ago.

"Oh, Evan might know something about it," Michael said offhandedly. "He's somewhat of an *expert* on pirates."

Evan threw his head back and laughed.

"That's not *funny*, Michael!" John said. Sofia was holding onto his arm, and John looked down at her apologetically. "It really isn't funny, you know," he told her with a shake of his head.

LATER THAT EVENING the group was gathered in the Darling's apartment. They were playing a lively game of Catch Phrase – boys against girls. Evan felt amazed that despite the fact that Italian was Gina and Sofia's primary language, the girls were winning. As they reached the final winning point, the girls clapped excitedly and high-fives were sent around.

"We let them win," John whispered loudly. "Right?" He looked between Evan and Michael.

Michael patted John's shoulder consolingly. "Sure," he said.

Gina and Sofia commented on the hour, but apparently Michael wasn't through with his time with Gina. He stood and extended his hand to help her up from the floor. "How about a walk?" he suggested. "It's a lovely evening." Gina blushed and took his hand, rising from the floor.

"Wonderful idea, Michael!" John said, beginning to stand. "Let's all go for a walk!"

Evan noticed Wendy shake her head as she tilted it back with exasperation. Apparently, she didn't agree. Why didn't she want to go, too? Was she tired of spending time with him?

"John," she said gently, "let's have the rest of us stay *here* while Gina and Michael go out *alone*." She gave him a meaningful look, eyes wide and head tilted slightly down.

John looked confused and gestured toward the door. "But, Michael's right – it's a nice night out..." he stopped talking when Wendy lifted her eyebrow. "Oh, alright." He turned to his date. "Sofia, have you ever played Uno?"

Michael escorted Gina out the door. Evan observed them holding hands.

"You've quite the persuasive abilities," Evan said quietly to Wendy once Michael and Gina had left. She smiled at him with apparent self-satisfaction. He was still confused as to her motives for not joining them on their walk. He looked from the door to Wendy. "So, why aren't we joining them?" he asked with mild confusion.

Then he remembered another thing he'd meant to ask her from earlier that day. "Also, what was with the 'breathtaking view,'" he used air quotes with his hand, "from the bridge that Michael talked about after the ride in the canyon?" He nodded his head toward outside.

Wendy pulled her lips in, stifling a giggle and trying to contain a smile. She looked over to where John and Sofia were setting up a game of Uno. She turned back to Evan and said quietly, "There's a song I love called 'Breathless.' Michael was referring to it when he said the view was 'breathtaking.' He and Gina took longer on their ride this afternoon because he kissed her on the bridge." She raised her eyebrows meaningfully.

Evan took a moment to put the pieces together, then his mouth formed a large "O." He nodded in understanding, reaching out to hold Wendy's hand. "So then," he surmised, "he's taking her on a walk to kiss her again." He tilted his head and waggled his eyebrows.

Wendy kissed his nose playfully. "You're a smart one, Evan Roberts," she teased.

"I think Michael is on to something," he responded. "Shall we go on a walk, too?"

## 27

I ndependence Day in Provo, Utah was spectacular – year after year. Provo took the holiday seriously. It began with an extensive, energetic parade going down University Avenue. Music, dancers, spotlights on local celebrities and businesses, school bands and cheerleaders – high energy throughout.

Then there was the Freedom Festival in Downtown Provo, which began a few days before the holiday, and continued through the holiday itself. There were tents with vendors selling everything from custom-made jewelry to custom-drawn pictures, specialty toys to specialty clothing. There were food stands with corn dogs, snow cones, popcorn, cotton candy, and the occasional taco stand. There were carnival rides that went up, down, fast, faster, around, backward, forward, sideways. And people were everywhere; the draw to the Freedom Festival was like a magnetic pull.

At the end of the day were fireworks – everywhere. Not only in Provo, but all over the valley. However,

Provo had its own special version of a fireworks show. The Stadium of Fire, which took place at BYU's LaVell Edwards Football Stadium, featured a concert prior to the fireworks show. Not just any sort of concert – well known music artists and other popular talents graced the stage, giving a rousing performance before the grand production of fireworks.

Wendy and Evan had decided to watch the fireworks from the vantage point of the mountain. They hiked to the Y, located on the mountain east of BYU campus ("Take LOTS of breaks on the trail!" John had warned). They watched the flashes of popping color scatter throughout the Utah Valley. The booming of fireworks echoed off the mountain.

Wendy sighed contentedly and leaned her head against Evan's shoulder. He wrapped his arm around her and let his head rest on hers. They sat in comfortable silence, taking in the sight.

As the fireworks began to die down across the valley, Wendy straightened, stretched her arms, and turned to Evan. "That was fun," she said. "I've never been up here to see that before." She really had enjoyed it, though the hike had her legs on fire halfway to the Y. *I'm going to be sore tomorrow*, she realized. *But it was worth it.*

Evan looked at Wendy. "Glad we didn't let John talk us out of it," he said, smirking.

Wendy imitated John's words and voice. "'It's crazy steep! Why don't you just drive up a hill to watch the fireworks, or something?'" She rolled her eyes. "He was right about the steepness," she said. "But it's worth the view." She looked back out over the valley.

Evan cricked his neck from side to side and stretched his legs in front of him. "What time is it?" he asked, looking back at Wendy.

"Oh! That's right!" she said as she pulled her watch out of her messenger bag. "We're supposed to meet everyone around 11:30 tonight." She hit the glow button on her watch, and it illuminated to show the time was 11:20 pm. She sighed in relief. "We're not late."

"Yet," Evan amended. "We still have to climb down this mountain and drive to the canyon." He tilted his head down and raised his eyebrows.

Wendy groaned. "I don't think I'll be able to walk tomorrow," she said. "I ought to hike more often to get used to it."

She squinted her eyes at Evan. "How is it that *you're* not sore or tired from all this?" she asked, waving a hand toward the trail.

He bent his knees and rested his elbows on them. Tilting his head to the side, he answered, "Wendy, I move furniture for a living. I carry heavy loads up and down stairs all the time." He nudged her with his elbow. "I'm used to stuff like this."

Wendy smirked. "Show off."

PETER LOOKED at the group assembled around the campfire. Some were roasting hot dogs, but most were roasting marshmallows. Thomas had been waxing philosophical on the proper way to roast a marshmallow, and Peter had tuned him out a few minutes ago.

But not out of anger or irritation. He was lost in thought, watching his friends.

There was Thomas, Slater, Coby, and Nick; John and Michael had brought their "friends," Sofia and Gina (though Peter believed that Michael and Gina had moved beyond the definition of "friends"); and Trina (who he hoped he could move beyond the definition of "friends" soon).

He could tell Trina was trying to show interest in Thomas's marshmallow soliloquy, but her adorable mind was either losing interest or wasn't following what Thomas was saying. She startled and yelped when she noticed that her marshmallow was on fire.

Peter quickly took the roasting stick from her hands and blew out the flame. He pulled the charred goo off the stick with a napkin and replaced it with a fresh mallow. Then he flipped the stick in the air and caught it while looking Trina in the eyes. Adoration bloomed all over her face; she blushed, clapped, and giggled a "Thank you" to him. He responded with a charming smile, warmth spreading through him at the sight of her happiness.

Peter had been seeing a counselor for several weeks to help him work through his issues. Wendy's professor had recommended a few potential professionals and Peter had found one he fit well with. The progress was coming steadily, though not overnight. But at this point, deliberately doing things to help others had begun to bring him a sense of happiness he hadn't known before. He wished he'd started doing it sooner.

Peter watched Thomas slowly roasting a mallow, caught the key movements, then reached out to help

Trina learn to do likewise. She scooted closer to him, and they held the stick together, with his hand resting on hers.

Thomas finally ended his mallow-speech and stuffed the toasted confection into his mouth.

"Do you think," John asked, "that roasting licorice would work, too?" He had a package of licorice in his lap and was attempting to skewer a piece onto his roasting stick. Sofia giggled from where she sat next to him, holding onto his arm with one of her hands. John looked down at her at the sound of her laugh. "What do you think?" he asked sincerely. She reached out and helped him secure the candy firmly, then John stuck it into the fire with a satisfied smile.

Coby was on his fourth s'more, bits of crumbs outlining his mouth.

Thomas must have noticed, and he looked puzzled. "How is it that you can eat like that and still maintain all that muscle?" he asked in confusion. He shook his head. "It goes against nature. Eating sweets and junk ought to have you looking flabby and soft, like me. Except I'm conscious of my sugar intake; I limit it whenever possible," he said superiorly. He pulled his second toasted mallow from his stick and stuffed it into his mouth.

Michael quietly snort laughed from across the circle.

Thomas looked over at him, a severe look on his face. "What?" he demanded, mouth full of mallow goo.

"Do you remember what Coby does for a living?" Michael asked, barely containing a smile and gesturing over to Coby.

Thomas's face screwed up in thought for several moments.

Coby answered the lingering question after swallowing the last of his s'more. "I move heavy stuff around all day, remember?"

Thomas still showed no signs of recognition, blinking slowly while chewing the mallow.

Peter couldn't take it anymore. He shook his head and said, "He works for a moving company, Thomas. He basically works out *all day*." He waved his hand at Coby. "He can afford to eat like that and still maintain that physique."

Coby lifted his fifth s'more in salute to Peter with a grin on his face.

"Though truly," Slater piped up, "you ought to draw the line somewhere with all those s'mores." He sent Coby a reprimanding but friendly look.

Coby shrugged and nodded. "I can stop. I don't want cavities, anyway."

Michael called over to Peter. "What time is it?" he asked, leaning around the fire to see Peter.

Peter glanced at his watch. "Just past 11:45," he answered, stretching his legs in front of him.

John looked at Michael. "She's late," he said to his brother, scowling slightly. "It's not like Wendy to be late."

"Oh!" Thomas exclaimed. "Is Wendy joining us this evening? I ought to have worn something nicer." He dusted off his khaki pants, incidentally smearing dirt and mallow residue from his hands.

Michael cleared his throat and all eyes focused on

him. He looked at John, then back at the group. "She's bringing a...friend." He glanced at Peter.

Peter nodded, one corner of his mouth lifting. He wouldn't ever be *friends* with Evan, but they didn't consider each other enemies anymore. "Common acquaintances" was a proper way to describe their relationship. Though even *that* was several huge strides of progress between them.

Thomas' excitement dimmed. "Oh," he said disappointedly. "She's dating someone, then?" he asked Michael. Michael nodded and shrugged at the same time.

Thomas sighed. "Well," he said, "I always knew she was too good for me, anyway." He straightened and put his roasting stick down, then his face brightened. "But," he continued, "there's a girl who often studies at the Law Library when I'm there. I've caught her sending smiles my way several times." He puffed his chest out and placed his hands on his legs. "I believe she's quite taken with me."

Nick and Slater snickered from where they sat next to Peter. Peter nudged them, trying to hide his own amused smile.

"What?" Thomas asked, incensed at their mocking. "I'm in law school; I'm quite the catch!" he defended while gesturing at his face.

Gina leaned toward Michael and whispered something in his ear. He nodded and smiled. "Gina says she has a friend she could set you up with," he said to Thomas, tilting his head at Gina.

"Oh?" Thomas asked, interest written all over his face.

Michael nodded. "Her friend is from France," he answered with an impressed look.

Thomas smacked his thigh with a "Ha!" Pointing to the rest of the group, he crowed. "Any of you lot ever date a girl from *France*?" he challenged with a triumphant look.

Peter glanced at his watch, resisting the urge to roll his eyes. Which the old-Peter would have done, followed by some snide comment. But he took a breath, held it for several seconds, and then let it slowly out.

Trina leaned in. "You okay?" she asked sincerely. That was one of the things he enjoyed about her company; she sincerely cared. He nodded and winked at her. She smiled and bit her lip, taking hold of his arm.

The group looked up and into the darkness as the sound of twigs breaking approached them. Seconds later Wendy's form showed in the light of the campfire. She approached with a large smile on her lovely face.

EVAN WATCHED from the shadows as Wendy approached the group, her feminine figure silhouetted in the firelight. Her friends' faces brightened at the sight of her. Shouts of "Wendy!" erupted from around the circle. People stood and hugged her. He smiled at the sight; Wendy brightened any environment she was in, but it was obvious that she was especially loved and appreciated by her brothers and their friends.

After several minutes of reunion someone asked her something. She glanced back at Evan, standing where he was in the darkness. She responded to the group, gesturing with her hands and pointing in Evan's general direction.

"Boyfriend?!" he heard someone protest. Evan chuckled to himself and smiled. It was a privilege to hold that title in relation to Wendy.

The group looked behind her, apparently trying to catch a glimpse of who she was pointing to. Wendy turned and smiled at him, waving him forward to join the group.

*Here goes nothing,* he thought.

NOW OR NEVER, Wendy told herself as she waved Evan toward the group. She was grateful that his identity would only be a shock to Thomas, Slater, and Nick. Peter, Coby, John, and Michael already knew – and had accepted – who Evan was.

Still a bit apprehensive, Wendy decided to preface Evan's approach. "You've all known him from *before*," she said cautiously. "But he's different from when you last saw him."

"What's that supposed to mean?" Thomas countered as Evan's footsteps drew nearer.

Wendy shrugged. "You'll see," she answered with a nervous smile.

Evan came from behind her, slipping his only hand into hers and giving it a quick squeeze. She looked up at him, relieved that he was there.

She heard a gasp and a thump and looked toward the group. Thomas had stumbled backwards and fallen down. Slater and Nick skittered behind Peter, likely out of an old habit. Each of their faces registered shock and confusion. Peter was the picture of calm and confidence; she hoped the others would catch on to his tranquility.

Then suddenly, "Hook!" Thomas yelled and pointed to Evan. "What are you doing here?" he asked, fear in his voice and written on his face.

Trina tsked. "Just because he's missing a hand doesn't mean you have to be all rude about it." She shook her head disdainfully.

Peter coughed and put his fist to his mouth, apparently hiding a laugh.

Evan looked down to hide a smirk and rubbed the back of his neck with his handless arm. His eyes scanned from Wendy to Peter, then to John, Michael, and Coby, each in turn. Coby smiled reassuringly and nodded to Evan with a thumbs-up.

Wendy cleared her throat with a meaningful glance at Thomas, hoping he would take the hint to calm down and be quiet.

"This is *Evan Roberts*," she stressed his name to leave no confusion about whether or not this was Captain Hook. She looked at Thomas, Slater, and Nick, with her eyebrow raised, daring them to contradict her. They'd always trusted her in Neverland; she hoped they would do so here.

"But..." Thomas began, pointing at Evan, "he looks just like—"

"Must be a doppelganger," Peter said quickly.

"Oh," was all Thomas said, appearing bewildered.

Peter sent a reassuring look to Thomas, Slater, and Nick, tilting his head toward Evan.

"Ohhhh!" all three friends said as realization dawned on them. Evan might be who they thought he was, but was no longer who he had been in the past.

Slater and Nick climbed forward from behind Peter, and Thomas stood from where he'd stumbled in shock, clearing his throat.

Michael piped in at this point. "Wendy's *hooked up* with quite the catch, don't you think?" He snickered at his joke, as did Peter, Evan, Wendy, and Coby.

John, however, was not amused. "That's *not funny*, Michael!" he said, irritated. He looked down at Sofia, whose arm was still wrapped adoringly around his. "It's just not funny," he said to her with a shake of his head. "Why does he keep doing that?" Sofia giggled and shrugged. She likely couldn't see why John was always so upset by Michael's jokes, but she seemed to admire John all the same when he reacted like that.

John scowled at his brother. Peter smacked his hand on his thigh and laughed. Michael snort laughed. Wendy sighed in relief and leaned her head against Evan's shoulder. That had all gone much better than she thought it would. The secret was out, but it was okay.

Wendy looked up at Evan. "Care for a marshmallow?" she asked playfully.

"If there are any left," Peter warned. "Between Coby and Thomas, I believe we may be out."

"Hey!" Thomas protested and scowled.

Coby laughed at the insinuation. "We've still got

one more bag we haven't busted open yet," he said, pointing to a package of marshmallows by his seat.

"Then I guess my answer is yes," Evan said, looking down at Wendy. "I would certainly care for a marshmallow." He looked up at the group. "Anyone know the best way to toast these?"

Peter laughed, pointing to Thomas. Between fits of chuckles he said, "Thomas here has an entire discourse on the art of marshmallow toasting. But maybe he could give you the *condensed* version." He cast Thomas a meaningful glance.

Thomas scowled at Peter but looked pleasantly at Evan. "Grab a roasting stick–" he began.

"Or a hook," Michael inserted with a snort laugh.

Thomas glared at Michael before he continued. "Make sure the end is clean; you don't want to eat a dirty marshmallow. That would be a waste of time and resources." He reached over to pick something up. "I've got some wet cloths here for just such a purpose. Now, choose the fluffiest mallow you can find. Yes, that one looks good. And gently wiggle it onto the end of the stick. No! Don't thrust it on! It'll poke a hole through the top and then it'll slide down the stick. Yes, that's better. Now..."

Thomas carried on for several minutes. Wendy noticed how patiently and obediently Evan humored Thomas and followed his instructions. And sure enough, he made a perfectly toasted marshmallow.

"Well done," Thomas praised. He looked around the group with an air of superiority. "Anything worth doing is worth doing well," he said insightfully.

Peter rolled his eyes but said nothing.

## 28

J uly rolled into August, and with August began Fall semester at BYU. Swarms of students filled the campus and the apartment complexes nearby. School supplies were in high demand, anticipation was elevated, and an excited energy permeated campus.

The first day of school had come and gone, and September began to showcase its colors as shades of red, orange, and yellow crept down the mountains, the fall season hinting at what was soon to come to the valley. The days were shorter, but the air still clung to summer-like temperatures. Students continued to wear warm weather outfits and footwear, dragging the style out as long as possible before the cold phase of fall would set in.

Wendy continued her work as Professor Brown's teacher's aide. She sat at her desk in his office, wearing her favorite denim knee-length skirt, a black cotton shirt tucked in, and black sandals to tie it together. She was hunched over the desk, studying for her own classes, as she had already finished her work grading papers for the day.

She heard the office door open but kept her eyes glued to the textbook. Assuming it to be the professor, she said, "The papers are all graded and resting on your desk, Professor."

"Professor, huh? I could get used to that," a familiar voice said, though it wasn't Professor Brown's.

Wendy's head shot up. A smile split her face. "Dave!" she exclaimed, jumping out of her seat and crossing the room quickly to give her friend a hug.

"It's been ages!" she said. She felt chagrin covering her features. "I'm sorry it's been so long since I've called!"

"Ages?!" Dave countered, looking surprised. "Girl, it's only been a couple months!" He swatted her arm playfully, smiling. "And you've been a bit *preoccupied...*" he dragged the word out slowly while raising both eyebrows.

Wendy rolled her eyes and swatted Dave back. "Yes," she confirmed, "Evan and I are a 'thing,' as you would call it." She giggled and folded her arms.

She looked around the office, suddenly realizing that seeing Dave in the Psychology department was out of place. "What are you doing here?" she asked with innocent curiosity.

"Oh!" Dave said, suddenly excited. "I'm taking Psych 101! I needed some more credits this semester, thought of you majoring in Psychology, and thought I'd give it a try." He spread his arms wide with a "Ta Da!"

Wendy clapped enthusiastically. "Good for you!"

she said. "I think you'll enjoy the class. Though, to be honest," she said, sobering for a moment, "you've probably already noticed that the teachers like to challenge your typical way of thinking."

Dave nodded, mouth scrunched. "Didn't see that coming," he admitted, adjusting his backpack.

"It takes some getting used to," Wendy agreed. "But you *do* get used to it. And then you see the world in a whole different way." She patted his arm, then clapped her hands together lightly in front of her. "I'm just so excited you're taking the class!"

Dave looked at her dubiously before smirking. "If you say so," he replied, pulling a chair closer to her desk and sitting down. Wendy followed suit, angling her chair to face her friend.

They sat talking, catching up and sharing stories, for almost an hour. One detail in particular caught Wendy's interest, and she couldn't help delving deeper with several questions.

"A girl from fencing gave you her number?!" she asked animatedly, excitedly tapping her feet on the floor.

Dave's huge grin showed the contrast of white teeth against his dark lips. "Heck yes, she did!" he exclaimed with a thrust of his head.

Wendy clapped giddily and squealed. "Who's the girl?" she asked as she placed her hand on his arm.

Dave gave a quick "Ha!" before continuing. "One of The Spice Girls we used to make fun of."

Wendy was bewildered for a few seconds. "The Spice...Oh!" Memory recall kicked in and she pictured the group of girls from their fencing class, the ones dressed in trendy, sparkly activewear with their hair in panda-ear buns.

"Oh, that's wonderful!" she responded. "Which girl from the group?" She felt genuinely excited for Dave, though she hoped it wasn't the ringleader of the group; that girl had always been a bit of a diva at class.

"The shy one," Dave answered. "The one with the green eyes and dark hair," he gestured to his eyes and head.

Wendy released the breath she'd held, relieved at his response. She raised her eyebrows and smiled. "She's a lovely girl," she said.

Dave straightened. "*Yeah* she is!" he said enthusiastically. "And apparently she's got the hots for me." He put his fists on his chest, as though holding onto imaginary suspenders, head raised proudly.

"I ran into her on campus about a week ago. We talked and all that, then she gave me her number." Dave did a lasso swing over his head while humming triumphantly.

Wendy laughed; she loved Dave's confidence. "Have you called her yet?" She continued to pry for information.

"Psh! Of course!" Dave exclaimed. "Called her that very night. Got a date lined up for this weekend and everything." He closed his eyes, apparently enjoying the reality of his situation. "Mmm, mmm, MMM!" he said, moving his head side to side. "Gonna be a *good* date!"

Wendy fist-bumped Dave, feeding off his energy and loving every second she had with him. They continued talking for a while longer before Dave checked his watch. His eyes widened and he yelped.

"Ah! I'm gonna be late for class!" He jumped up and reached his hand out to help Wendy up as well. He gave her a quick hug. "I'll be back again; promise!" he called as he trotted toward the door.

Wendy folded her arms contentedly as she watched him exit the room in a rush. Wondering just what time it was, she glanced up at the wall clock in the office. Her eyes widened and she gave a yelp of her own. "I'm going to be late meeting Peter!" she exclaimed out loud. She quickly collected her things, slipped her bag across her body, and jogged out the door.

PETER WAS DETERMINED to be on time for his meeting with Wendy. Punctuality showed respect, and if anyone deserved respect it was Wendy. They had reinstated their monthly meeting at the Harris Fine Arts Center, located near the heart of campus.

He rushed into the building, slowing down once he was a few steps inside. He quickly took stock of all the benches to see if Wendy had arrived before he had. He heaved a sigh of relief. *I'm early!* he realized.

He walked toward a bench flanked on either side by student-made art. His gait could no longer be called a swagger, though his strides still held self-assurance. Counseling had been humbling, and it showed in the way he held himself.

Peter was still intelligent, agile, and as fiercely good-looking as ever. It no longer went to his head, though.

He stopped flirting with every girl that walked past. What he *did* do was try to make girls feel respected instead of ogled.

He also made an effort to pay attention and work harder in his classes. Choosing the right major to study had made the effort much more enjoyable. Recreation Management had the potential to be an adventurous major.

He checked the time on his watch, then looked up at the entrance. Sure enough, Wendy entered right on time. And she looked lovely, as always. He saw her glance around at the benches, and Peter waved his hand in the air to make her search easier. Her face lit up when she spotted him. She waved back, picking up speed as she headed over.

He stood to greet her, gesturing to the bench for her to sit first.

"Such good manners," Wendy said as she sat down, putting her bag next to her.

Peter feigned incredulity, putting his hand to his chest. "Has it ever been otherwise?" he asked with a wink.

Wendy chuckled and patted the seat next to her. Peter sat and reached to give her a friendly hug. "How are you, Wendy?" he asked as they pulled out of the hug.

They talked back and forth, discussing the semester so far, work, and the relationships they were in.

Wendy's smile grew wide. "How's Trina?" she asked with delight while tapping her feet on the floor.

Peter sat up straighter and rubbed his hands together. "She's fantastic," he answered with a genuine smile. "She's become a shift manager at work, which means Outdoors Unlimited is in good hands." Despite being a bit air-headed, Trina was a hard worker. "Which also means," Peter continued, waggling his eyebrows, "that I get scheduled to work her shift each week."

To Peter, the only thing better than working at Outdoors Unlimited was being able to work with Trina at Outdoors Unlimited.

Wendy's face brightened, sharing his enthusiasm. "That's great news – for both of you!"

"I know," Peter enthused back. "She always giggles in that adorable way of hers when we pass each other at work. And we only make out in the back a *few* times a week." He shrugged and side-glanced at Wendy to catch her reaction.

Wendy gasped, then laughed. "Peter!" She tried to swat his shoulder.

His reflexes, swift as always, blocked her swat. "I'm only joking!" he laughed while deflecting her continual attempts to hit him.

Wendy ceased her futile swatting at his confession. "Good," she said. "If someone caught you two back there..." she reprimanded.

Peter rolled his eyes but smiled. "Alright, we don't make out at work," he said. "But we *do* make out." He smiled and crossed his arms over his chest.

Wendy snort laughed, covered her nose and mouth with her hands, eyes wide at her snort, then burst out laughing after Peter started laughing at her snort.

*This is so much better than last spring*, Peter thought. Wendy was genuinely happy, they weren't arguing, his whole focus was on her, and things felt naturally well between them.

Peter reflected on how much had changed. He supposed if he had straightened himself out months – even years – ago that he might have had a chance at a romantic relationship with Wendy. It would've been amazing, because Wendy was an amazing woman.

But so was Trina. And Wendy was so well-suited with Evan. Peter brushed aside all the might-have-beens and embraced the reality of his life. And he was happy.

## 29

The promise of fall was being fulfilled as September progressed. Leaves in the valley morphed from their summer-green into bright hues of red, orange, and yellow. Quaking Aspen trees shimmered like gold coins whenever a breeze carried through their leaves. The air turned chilly enough for cardigans, sweatshirts, and the like. Corn mazes and haunted houses opened up as September became October. And fall was suddenly in full swing.

Evan wandered through a pumpkin patch, locally owned and operated by a farmer and his family. In Evan's hand he held a simple diamond ring in a velvet box. He scanned the assortment of pumpkins, looking for one with a slender enough stem for the ring to slip onto.

He decided to enlist the help of the farmer who, after hearing Evan's plan, gladly aided him in the search. Two heads are better than one, and within a short time they had found the perfect pumpkin.

Evan made arrangements with the farmer regarding the ring and the pumpkin and told the farmer he would return the next afternoon. He tried to pay the farmer extra for his help, but the man only smiled and shook his head, saying the experience ahead would be priceless to observe.

~

THE NEXT DAY, Evan sat in the passenger's seat of the moving van. He kept running his hand through his hair then rubbing the back of his neck. He was nervous.

Coby cleared his throat as they headed to their first moving job of the day. "You okay?" he asked while glancing at Evan. His anxious vibe was apparently obvious to Coby.

Evan stared ahead mutely for a moment before it registered that Coby had spoken. Quickly glancing between Coby and the road ahead, Evan responded with an ambiguous "Hmm?"

Coby chuckled, his voice deep and strong as ever. "Your head's in the clouds, dude." He shook his head and continued to chuckle.

Evan's head flicked over to Coby. "What?" he challenged. "What do you mean 'in the clouds'?" he asked with a confused look.

Coby shook his head again. "You're out to lunch, spacing out, head in the clouds," he explained. "You've never heard those things before?" he asked with one eye squinted dubiously.

"Oh!" Evan said with a jolt. "You mean to say I'm distracted. Right?"

Coby nodded. "Bingo."

Evan realized he hadn't caught many American colloquialisms despite his having lived there for a few years. He adjusted his position in his seat, feeling hesitant to answer Coby. "I'm..." he began. "I'm fine," his voice broke a bit at the end of his answer.

Coby gave a friendly laugh. "Evan," he said, "you are *so* thinking about Wendy, aren't you?"

Evan smiled and glanced at Coby. "Maybe..." he dragged the word out.

Coby smiled wide and thumped the steering wheel. "Knew it!" he crowed.

He turned to Evan, suddenly looking confused. "Okay, but, why are you so nervous?" he asked. "I've seen you distracted thinking about her, but never, like, *nervous*-distracted thinking about her." He appeared worried. "Are the two of you ok?"

Evan's face sobered. "Oh! Yes, we're doing well," he reassured, casting a smile quickly in Coby's direction. "Seriously well," he continued. He smiled bigger. "Really seriously well. *Extremely* really seriously well." His felt his smile grow with each sentence.

"My friend," Coby said with a smirk, "you're so 'extremely really seriously' smitten," he teased.

Evan raised his eyebrows in sobriety. "Yes, I am," he said seriously. He rolled his shoulders, kinked his neck side to side, and repeated the nervous gestures he'd done earlier – running his hand through his hair, rubbing the back of his neck...

Coby shook his head. "I'm still in the dark here, Evan. Help me out."

Evan inhaled a breath and let it out slowly to calm

his anxiousness. Coby pulled to a stop in front of their destination.

"We're here," Evan said, trying to change the subject. He unbuckled his seat to exit the van, but Coby put a hand on Evan's arm before either of them could leave.

Coby looked imploringly at Evan. "Hey," he said quietly. "You can tell me." He raised his eyebrows and tilted his chin down sincerely.

Evan's heartbeat raced at the thought of sharing his thoughts with someone. But Coby was a trusted friend. He would be a good person to speak to.

Evan took another deep breath and let it out in a quick huff. He turned in his seat to face Coby, drumming his fingers on his thigh. Looking up at Coby, he confessed, "I love Wendy."

Coby stared at Evan, apparently waiting for something more revelatory than what he'd just heard. "And...?" he asked with an expectant look.

Evan was a little shocked that Coby wasn't shocked by his confession. "You don't sound surprised," he answered with a half-smile.

"Evan," Coby said straightforwardly, "it's pretty obvious to everyone how you feel about her. Why would I be surprised?" He shrugged.

"Oh," Evan said, tilting his head to the side and looking out the front window. He guessed it wasn't a *bad* thing that his feelings for Wendy were evident to those around them. But then—

"Do you think *Wendy* knows how I feel about her?" Evan asked anxiously.

Coby smirked. "She'd have to be slower than me

not to," he said honestly, landing a light punch on Evan's shoulder.

Evan laughed at Coby's answer, then ran his hand through his hair again.

"So, um," Coby said while tapping his fingers on his seat, "what're you gonna do about it?" he asked shyly.

Evan straightened and rolled his shoulders back. He looked at Coby and raised his eyebrows. "I'm going to ask her to marry me," he declared.

Coby's jaw dropped open, his eyes widening at the same time. "Whoa!" he exclaimed. "That's *awesome!*" He pulled Evan into a Coby-size hug (much like a bear hug – tight and enveloping). "Congrats!"

"Thank you," Evan wheezed out.

"Oh," Coby said, releasing Evan from the strong hold. "Sorry. But, like, not sorry at the same time." His face brightened and he clapped his hands. "I'm so excited for you!" he said, his voice raising with each word. It was the giddiest Evan had ever seen Coby – in the real world or in Neverland.

Evan barked out a laugh and shook his head. "I haven't asked her yet," he said, his breathing suddenly shallow. He ran his hand through his hair once again.

Realization dawned on Coby's features. "Oh!" he cried. "You're so nervous because you're going to ask her *soon.*"

Evan let out a long breath and smiled. "Yes, soon. And I'm terrified," he admitted as he slid his hand down his face.

Coby regarded Evan for several moments. "You're gonna do just fine, Evan," he reassured. "There's no way she'll say no."

"But what if she does?" Evan asked with slight panic.

"She won't," Coby reiterated, shaking his head. He patted the steering wheel. "We better get started," he said. "And we can talk some more while we go."

Evan gave a quick nod. Not because he was anxious to get started with the moving job, but because a resolute calm had settled over him at Coby's reassurances.

Evan could do this. He *would* do this. And he would ask Wendy tonight.

∾

"T<small>RY</small> to find some of the big, round ones," John instructed Wendy. He held his hands wide apart, indicating how "big and round" he meant. "Those make the best jack-o-lanterns!"

Wendy, John, and Michael sat in the front room of their apartment. Deciding to take a break from studying, they'd begun discussing Wendy's plans with Evan for the evening. He'd said something about getting pumpkins, and John apparently had requests.

Wendy nodded at John's statement. "Those *do* tend to make for a good jack-o-lantern," she agreed.

Michael quirked an eyebrow. "They also tend to have more innards to extract." He made a face and stuck his tongue out.

"Oh, I'd forgotten," John said. "Michael hates gutting the pumpkins." He put his hand to his chin, looking thoughtfully at the floor. Suddenly, "I've got it!" he said, pointing his index finger. "Wendy and I," he waved between himself and Wendy, "will clean out the insides of the pumpkins, and Michael can help carve the faces. That way we can *still* get the biggest ones and Michael won't get sick carving pumpkins this year." He put his hands on his hips and beamed at his brother.

A corner of Michael's lips lifted, and he patted his brother on the arm. "That's a great idea, John," he said as he stood to stretch. "And I appreciate your thoughtfulness."

John nodded. "It's settled, then," he said, turning to Wendy. "And we can help carry the pumpkins from Evan's car if you need us to."

Wendy giggled at John's enthusiasm. Fall was his favorite season, and his love of it was contagious. "We'll do our best to find the right pumpkins, John," she reassured with a smile.

There was a knock on the door. "I'll get it!" John jumped from his spot and trotted over to answer it. "It's Evan!" he called over his shoulder.

Wendy walked over and stood next to John in the doorway, slightly shooing him away. "Go back to studying," she whispered loudly with a pointed look.

"Oh! Right!" John said. And with that, he joined Michael in the front room.

Wendy turned to Evan, holding the door open wider. "Do you want to come in before we go?" she asked.

Evan stared at her, a panicked expression on his face.

Wendy glanced into the apartment, then looked back at him. "Evan," she said, stepping outside and closing the door behind her. "Are you ok?" She put her hands on his arms and looked up at his face with worry.

Evan snapped out of his staring and looked down at Wendy. "Sorry. I'm alright," he said reassuringly. He cupped her face with his hand and looked at her adoringly.

*I love this feeling*, Wendy thought to herself. *I love feeling loved.*

Evan's feelings for Wendy were obvious. It was evident in how he interacted with her, how he looked at her, how he treated her, how he spoke with her, how he listened to her, how he apologized when he upset her, how he held her. Wendy hoped her feelings for Evan were as conspicuous as his were for her.

He slid his hand into hers, holding it securely, then flicked his head toward his car. "Let's go find some pumpkins," he said with a half-smile.

Wendy laughed on the way to the car as she explained John's instructions about finding the right pumpkins. Evan chuckled as he opened Wendy's door for her.

She paused before getting in. Looking up at Evan she said simply, "Thank you."

Evan squinted one eye and quirked an eyebrow. "For what?" he asked.

Wendy sighed contentedly. "For taking good care of me," she answered, smirking at how adorable he was when he was curious.

"My pleasure," he said, giving her a dramatic bow.

Wendy laughed as she slid into the passenger seat. He was adorable when he bowed, too. Actually, the more accurate word would be that he was dashing when he acted the gentleman. The modern phrase would be, "It's hot when he does that." Wendy agreed with that vernacular wholeheartedly. Her heart picked up speed at the thought.

THE PUMPKIN PATCH was fairly well populated for it being a weekday. People milled around the rows of pumpkins, organized by size of small, medium, large, and extra-large. There were tables with boxes of smaller pumpkins suitable for baking. There were hay bales stacked for photo opportunities. The crowd was varied and diverse – families with young children, groups of teenagers, older couples, pairs of younger couples.

Wendy loved the feel of the slight chill in the air. She hugged Evan's arm closer to warm herself up as they perused the row of extra-large pumpkins.

Evan pointed to one. "Would that one be John-approved?" he asked with a teasing smile.

Wendy giggled. "Maybe," she answered. "But let's keep looking. I think he's picturing something bigger than that."

They continued to stroll, their heads turning left and right to survey the options. Wendy jumped when she saw a pumpkin the size of a large tire. "That one!" she said, pointing to it.

Evan turned to see where she pointed. "Whoa!" he exclaimed. It truly was enormous. "If that doesn't satisfy John's standards for size," he said with a shake of his head, "then tell him to go find one himself."

Wendy nudged Evan, a snort laugh escaping in the process.

"As strong as you are, I don't think even *you* will be able to carry that to the car," Wendy said. "Do you think we'll even be able to carry it together?" she asked dubiously.

Evan pointed toward the main building of the pumpkin patch. "They have some wheelbarrows back there," he said. "We can heft it up then wheel it to the car."

"Oh, good," Wendy said with a relieved sigh. She looked back at the pumpkin. "That thing is enormous."

Evan nudged Wendy. "What about you?" he asked.

"What *about* me?" she asked curiously.

"What sort of pumpkin do *you* want?" he answered, eyebrows slightly furrowed.

Wendy shrugged. "I'm not sure," she said. "I was just going by John's instructions." She did a mock-salute, making Evan laugh.

He pulled on her hand. "Let's go get a wheelbarrow and load this monstrosity, then we can go see if the farmer has any suggestions for us," he said.

"Oh, okay," Wendy said, though inwardly she was hesitant to ask for outside opinions. She and Evan could choose any pumpkin they wanted now that they'd found one to satisfy John.

They secured a wheelbarrow, hefted the ginormous pumpkin onto it ("If this isn't up to John's standards, I'm making *him* return it!" Wendy had said after the strenuous activity) and took it to Evan's car after paying for it at the main building. The immense gourd barely fit into the back seat of the car.

Then they went in search of the farmer, but it didn't take long. Ever since they'd gotten the wheelbarrow he'd hovered near the main building, watching them.

*Maybe he's just a curious man and not trying to be creepy*, Wendy thought, giving him the benefit of the doubt.

Evan shook hands with the farmer and asked if he might help them find a pumpkin suitable for Wendy.

The farmer looked between Wendy and Evan, a knowing smile on his face. "I've got just the one," he said, nodding. He turned and went into the building, disappearing as the door closed behind him.

"What odd behavior," Wendy said. She looked at Evan quizzically. "Why do you suppose he went into the building? All the pumpkins are outside." She waved her hand toward the assortment of gourds.

Evan's lips pursed together, trying to hide a smile. Then he shrugged. "I guess we'll see," was all he said.

Wendy eyed him skeptically. "I guess we will."

Moments later the farmer returned, carrying a large cardboard box with a lid.

*A box?* Wendy wondered.

The farmer strode over to Evan and handed the box to him.

"Anything else I can help with?" the farmer asked with a meaningful look.

"I'll take it from here," Evan answered, smiling larger.

Wendy looked between the two of them. Then she noticed that some of the pumpkin patch employees had congregated near the building. The farmer attempted to shoo them away as he walked toward them, but in the end, he stood next to them.

And they were all watching Evan and Wendy.

*What on earth?*

She looked up at Evan, who seemed to be holding his breath. He released it in a quick sigh, locking eyes with Wendy.

"You remember," he began, shifting his hold on the box. "You remember how you said that I take good care of you?"

"Yes..." Wendy said, drawing out the word. "What's in the box, Evan?" she asked with a half-smile.

Instead of answering, Evan lowered the box to the ground and knelt beside it. He pulled off the lid; there was indeed a pumpkin inside. Evan lifted it from the box and held it in front of him. Then he shifted one foot so that he was kneeling down *on one knee.*

*Hold on!* Wendy thought, a jolt shooting through her body.

Evan held the pumpkin out. As the afternoon daylight landed on the pumpkin, a sparkle caught Wendy's eye from the stem. Her eyes widened and her hands shot to her mouth. There on the stem was a diamond ring.

Wendy gasped as tears sprang to her eyes and her pulse raced. She looked down at Evan, who was absolutely beaming with pride.

"Wendy," he said her name adoringly. "I love you. I want to take care of you, *forever.*"

Tears ran down Wendy's face. She moved one hand to cover her heart, which pounded in anticipation.

"Will you marry me?" Evan asked, his expression imploring, anxious, and nervous.

Wendy was already nodding before he could finish. "Yes," she choked out. Then, "Yes!" she exclaimed, pulling her hands from her mouth and chest, and putting them on either side of Evan's face.

Evan pumped his handless arm in the air with a shout of "Woo!" He jumped up, still holding the pumpkin, and kissed her soundly.

Shouts and cheers erupted from all around them. Wendy laughed against Evan's lips. "You and the farmer were in on this together, weren't you?" she murmured.

Evan pulled back and winked at her. Then, holding the pumpkin in one arm, he gently removed the ring from the stem and placed it on Wendy's ring finger.

She held it closer, loving how it glittered in the sunlight from every angle. It was a simple solitaire diamond, but to Wendy, it was amazing how much joy was contained in such a small object.

She looked at Evan, who nodded toward the crowd. "Better show them," he said.

Wendy raised her left hand and waved it around. The cheering and clapping grew louder until the farmer intervened by shouting, "Okay, folks! Let's leave 'em alone now!"

Wendy laughed and bit her lip, turning back to Evan. He looked at her lips, groaned, and pulled her close to kiss her again. Wendy ran her ring-bedecked hand through his hair, loving the feel of it.

∿

EVAN AND WENDY pulled up to her apartment, and he wished they had a wheelbarrow handy. John's pumpkin was too big for the two of them to heft alone.

They looked at each other, then Wendy held out her left hand and wiggled her fingers. Evan reached out, took her hand, and kissed the back of it. He couldn't wait until he had a ring on his left hand, too. He was suddenly grateful that Peter had cut off his right hand instead of his left.

The thought had him laughing out loud, head tossed back.

"What's got you so amused?" Wendy giggled with him.

Evan shared his thoughts with her. Wendy shook her head trying to hide a smile but failed.

"Of all the things to be grateful for," she snickered. She tilted her head to the side in thought. With a look of resignation and a shrug of her shoulders she said, "I suppose a ring wouldn't stay on a hook very well, now, would it? So it really *is* a blessing he got your right hand."

Evan laughed harder.

"What?" Wendy asked innocently.

"Just your logic," Evan answered once he'd gotten his laughter in check. "A ring on a hook truly *wouldn't* stay on very well; especially since my hook is gone." He winked, then opened his door to exit the car.

They entered the apartment to find John and Michael still at the academic grindstone, textbooks and notebooks open in front of them.

John looked up. "Wendy!" He snapped his books shut and jumped from his seat on the couch. Rubbing his hands together with excitement, he asked, "So, what did you find?" He looked between the two of them expectantly.

Wendy exchanged an amused look with Evan.

"We found your pumpkin," Evan answered. "And it's so big that we'll need both of you to help us get it inside." He gestured to John and Michael.

John did a happy dance to the chant of "Pump-kin! Pump-kin!"

"Well," John addressed them after he'd finished, "let's go get it!"

"Hang on," Wendy interjected before John could bolt out the front door. "We also found something sparkly while we were there." She had her hands clasped behind her back.

Michael's head perked up from his textbook. John stood where he'd stopped mid-stride on his way to the door. He tapped his foot impatiently. "Well," he said, "quickly tell us what you found, then let's go get the pumpkin!"

Wendy did the shoulder-swaying thing she did when she was happy. Then she swung her left hand forward, displaying her engagement ring.

"I knew it!" Michael shouted, jumping up from his seat.

John stood there with a dumbfounded expression. He looked from the ring to Wendy, to Evan, and back to the ring. A huge smile spread across his face. He flung his arms out. "Congratulations!" he exclaimed.

The brothers enveloped Wendy in a huge hug, which was followed by hearty handshakes with Evan.

John declared that studying was over for the day and that a celebration was in order.

And so, they celebrated the happy news of their sister and her fiancé, and the pumpkin was no longer a priority. (Though at the end of the evening it really did take all four of them to get the colossal thing inside.)

## 30

As many BYU college students who get engaged do, Evan and Wendy set their wedding date between semester breaks. Feeling that Christmas break was too soon to pull everything together (though students had been known to put a wedding in place within a couple months of getting engaged), they decided to wait until April.

Peter, who had been elated at the news of the engagement, had suggested a quick Vegas marriage. Wendy thought he was joking, but he was entirely serious.

"Why wait?" he'd said. "Just go and make it official. Then you can honeymoon there right after." His idea had been turned down, but it hadn't seemed to bother him. "Suit yourselves," he'd said.

Spring was a lovely time of year for a wedding. And having six months to plan and prepare had been just right for Wendy and Evan.

Not having many close female friends, Wendy had

asked Gina, Sofia, and Trina to accompany her dress shopping. And while at first, she questioned her judgement in asking them, the trips to the dress shops had been surprisingly fun.

And successful. Gina and Sofia had excellent taste in fashion, and Trina was honest to a fault when telling Wendy how she looked in the dresses she tried on. All in all, the experience was made better with the extra help.

Her wedding dress was white; lace sleeves extended to her wrists; a square neck accentuated her delicate collarbone; the corset bodice hugged her slender waist, with laces tying the back; the skirt flowed down to the floor in layered waves, alternating between lace and satin fabric.

Wendy thought Evan looked quite dapper in his black tuxedo.

And, apparently, she wasn't the only one who thought so. When Evan entered the chapel, Wendy overheard Trina whisper loudly to Peter, "Oh, wow! He looks HOT!" Her comment was followed by a snort laugh from Peter.

The marriage ceremony was simple and beautiful. Cheering and clapping ensued when the newlyweds presented themselves to those gathered, and the reception followed.

Almost everyone they knew well were in attendance, as well as acquaintances. The group of friends from the Monday night activities; some of Evan's former fencing students, including Dave (who arrived with the Spice Girl he'd been dating for several months); friends from Wendy's classes; Professor

Brown, whom she still worked for; Wendy's brothers, with Gina and Sofia; Peter, with Trina; and Nick, Slater, Coby, and Thomas.

Though at first Thomas was missing in action. His friends kept watch on the time, commenting on how Thomas was *never* late to anything.

Then suddenly he entered the venue with an insanely gorgeous woman on his arm. The former Lost Boys all dropped their jaws at the sight, wondering out loud who the girl was and how on earth Thomas had landed a date with her.

Gina and Sofia giggled, explaining that this was their French friend they'd promised to set Thomas up with.

Thomas approached his friends proudly, chest puffed out and eyebrows raised. He introduced his date, botching her French name terribly. She giggled and cuddled herself closer to Thomas. When Thomas had seemingly had his fill of showing off his date, he steered her toward the refreshment table, leaving his friends in his wake, scratching their heads in bewilderment.

As the evening approached its end, Evan, Wendy, her brothers, and their friends (and dates) were the only ones remaining. John brought up the topic of the honeymoon location, as it had been a secret Evan was to surprise Wendy with.

"I know!" John said mischievously, rubbing his hands together. "You're taking her on a cruise *ship!*" He looked around the group, apparently anticipating laughter. "Get it?! Pirate, and a ship! What?"

Michael approached his brother, patting him on the

shoulder. "I'm proud of you for finally making a pirate joke, John." Then he shook his head. "But as you would say, 'That's not funny.' Because in all honesty, that was a lame joke."

John looked irritated. "But it's always funny when *you* make those jokes!" he argued.

"That's because I don't make them lame," Michael said with a wink, patting John's arm again.

John huffed and turned to the group. "Well, I meant to tell a lame joke," he said. "I was just trying to lighten the mood and all that."

Sofia giggled, stood on tiptoe, and kissed John's cheek.

His face turned red, and he smiled from ear to ear. He cleared his throat. "I think," he said to the group, "that Sofia and I will go take a *walk*." He waggled his eyebrows exaggeratedly and tugged Sofia toward the exit, with her giggling girlishly all the way out. She glanced over her shoulder and gave a thumbs-up to Gina, who returned the gesture with enthusiasm.

Michael snort laughed. "Not one for subtlety, is he?" Gina playfully swatted Michael's chest. "What?" he asked.

WHILE THE FOCUS was on John's blunderous joke, Evan tugged on Wendy's arm. She looked up at him, and he cocked his head to a side exit. Wendy nodded, and the two slipped out of the venue together.

Their bags had already been packed and stowed in Evan's car for their honeymoon trip. He had told her to pack for somewhere tropical, but Wendy still didn't know where they were going.

After quickly changing into street clothes, they drove to the Salt Lake City airport. When they arrived at the terminal Wendy saw their destination was the Caribbean. Her jaw dropped and she felt happily shocked.

Evan laughed at her response. "John was spot on," he commented, reaching out to take Wendy's hand.

"Spot on about..." Wendy said, feeling confused.

"About a cruise ship," Evan answered with an amused smile.

It took Wendy a moment to connect John's lame joke with Evan's comment, and then she was in a fit of giggles.

After checking in and finding a seat, while waiting for their flight, Wendy leaned over and asked, "Why the Caribbean?" She tucked an errant lock of hair behind her ear.

Evan's brows furrowed in concern. "You don't want to go there?" he asked.

"Of course I want to go there!" she said reassuringly, leaning closer to Evan. "I just wondered if there was a specific reason." She put her face in her hand and rested her elbow on her knee.

Evan smirked playfully.

"What is it?" Wendy asked, smirking back.

"Remember the movie about the *pirates* in the Caribbean?" he answered with a mischievous smile and a raised brow.

Wendy threw her head back and laughed. "You will

*never* live this down!" she exclaimed after reclaiming her breath from laughing.

Evan crossed his arms in satisfaction and leaned back in his seat, one ankle crossed over the other knee. "John will never let up that he guessed right about the cruise..." Evan began.

"And Michael will never let it die about the pirate connection," Wendy finished with a huffed laugh.

# EPILOGUE

The once-inhabitants of Neverland continued their lives, building on their foundation of a new start.

The former Lost Boys pursued their careers, succeeding in their endeavors.

John dated Sofia, taking things slower than she would have liked, but they enjoyed their experiences together.

Michael took things to a higher level with Gina as they began to talk of marriage the following Fall semester, much to her delight.

Peter continued to see a counselor, progressed in making positive changes in his life, and continued to date Trina, with the hope and aim that he might one day spend the rest of his life with her.

Evan and Wendy built their new life together in the real world as husband and wife, grateful for the second chance life had given them.

As for Happily Ever After, the lives of our Never-land friends weren't perfect. Just as life isn't perfect for anyone. But they chose happiness, and so they lived happily.

*The End*

# ACKNOWLEDGMENTS

This story was crazy fun to write, but it wouldn't be where it is now without a lot of help.

Extraordinary thanks to each of my fabulous beta readers – you helped me polish this book into an immensely more readable version that it might have been. It was such a joy to work with each of you!

Thank you to the many helpers and supporters from the following Facebook groups: Moms Who Write, The Writing Gals Critique Group, Supporting Beginner Writers, and Indie Author Support Group. You guys are awesome!

Thanks also to the talented Anjanee from 17 Studio Book Design. We wouldn't have the beautiful cover without your artistic vision.

My editor, Celia Pool, just rocks. Thank you for your incredible expertise and considerable patience while going through my manuscript.

Hooray for my thesaurus app! Thank you for the synonym rolls – just like grammar used to make.

I'm so grateful for my anything-but-a-pirate husband, Andy, for cheering me on throughout this whole process, and for listening to my random thoughts and ideas that make absolutely no sense.

And finally, I give thanks to God for His blessings and guidance. He is the giver of all good things.

# ABOUT THE AUTHOR

Mindy LeMieux earned a Bachelor of Science degree at Brigham Young University in Provo, Utah. She enjoys reading, spending time with family, traveling, baking, and listening to Owl City. She currently lives in Utah with her husband, four kids, two cats, and one healthy supply of chocolate. You can follow her shenanigans on Instagram.

CPSIA information can be obtained
at www.ICGtesting.com
Printed in the USA
BVHW082053050622
638965BV00006B/136

9 780578 293950